HAUNTED HEART

HAUNTED HEART

THE THREE FEARS OF FAITH

JERRY HUMPHREY

WESTBOW
PRESS
A DIVISION OF THOMAS NELSON

WestBow Press books may be ordered through booksellers or by contacting:

WestBow Press
A Division of Thomas Nelson
1663 Liberty Drive
Bloomington, IN 47403
www.westbowpress.com
1-(866) 928-1240

ISBN: 978-1-4497-9664-8 (sc)

Library of Congress Control Number: 2013909606

Printed in the United States of America.

WestBow Press rev. date: 05/31/2013

The scariest place doesn't house monsters—it houses sin.

SPECIAL DEDICATIONS

I dedicate this book to Christ my Lord, who makes this all possible – not just because He gave me the desire, drive and determination to write – but because my heart burns to bring biblical perspective.

I also dedicate this book to my wife and kids. To my wife, Jasmine: Thank you for believing in me. It means more to me than you know. I love you. To my kids (Chesarai, Chavez, Jabez, Jerry, Jr. III (Bop), Jeremiah and Ezra: Without you guys, this book wouldn't even exist. Thank you. You brought this book to life.

Lastly, I would like to dedicate this book to my dad (Gerald N. Humphrey, Sr.), my mom (Toni J. Thomas) and my sister (J. Vanessa Humphrey). Thank you all for your constant, undying encouragement. I love you.

INTRO

If you love suspense—never knowing what's going to happen next—you're really going to enjoy this story. It's an adventure like no other. Nothing is as it seems.

Its three brothers verses one really dark, spooky house. Typically entering a haunted house is a challenge given by neighborhood friends or some strange man with one-eye, but not the case in this book.

While it may seem this story is about fear, it's really about courage. This haunted house challenge isn't just some silly way to prove you're tough, but a challenge that tests what you're *really* made of. So ask yourself, 'What are you *really* made of?' Get ready for the scariest story ever told.

CHAPTER 1

THE GREATEST TREAT

Today is Halloween Day—October 31, 2010. I love this time of year because the church we attend doesn't ignore it like most churches do. Our church is loaded with kids. I guess it'd be pretty hard to ignore a holiday that attracts so many children with candy of all kinds—tootsie rolls, sweet tarts, sugar babies, Now-and-Laters, Smarties, tootsie pops, Dots, Milk Duds, Hershey's miniatures (Krackels, Mr. Goodbar and Hershey's milk chocolate), popcorn balls, candy apples, candy corn (autumn mix) and Mike and Ike's.

No, our church never handed us all those sugary treats, but it certainly made up for it with a great alternative. Let me tell you about our teacher at church.

Mrs. Paraclete is the best Church teacher of all time. She is our Bible teacher for our class on Sundays. Every Sunday she gives us Bible memory verses to remember. If we remember our verses, she always gives us a treat.

Mrs. Paraclete is a very nice teacher—very soft-spoken. She only raises her voice if she really has to and you hardly ever catch her without a smile on her face. As we enter the classroom, she stands right outside the room greeting us with warm hugs and handshakes.

She always wears long white or light-colored dresses. The light colors seem to really add to the joy she brings to our class. Her hair is normally pulled up in a bun held together by a fancy hairpiece of some kind.

She looks really young, but no one knows how old she is. Any time anyone asks her how old she is, especially when her birthday comes around, she always says, "Now you know you never ask a lady her age," but then she'd follow up and jokingly say, "And besides, you know age *ain't* nothing but a number."

One year, a smart-witted kid spoke up and said, "Well, we'll rephrase the question: What *number* are you?"

Laughing back with her much wittier response, she replied, "My number is 9,375. Now you have to determine if that is years, days or months." Every time she says that, we laugh hopelessly knowing she is not going to tell us her age. We would need four calculators and a mathematician to figure out how old—*o excuse me*—what *number* she is.

Anyway, this Sunday was particularly special. It happened to be a Sunday that fell on October 31, Halloween Day. Also, this Sunday was different from our usual routine in class. Now she normally didn't do what I'm about to say, but Mrs. Paraclete decided to actually tell us what treat we'd get next Sunday if we memorized our memory verse. She promised to give us a combination of chocolate pudding, Oreo cookies with gummy worms on top—better known as a JELL-O Dirt Cups. Mmmm…so good, I thought to myself.

We never knew what treat Mrs. Paraclete would bring in for those of us who memorized our Bible memory verse. Knowing what the treat would be sparked more excitement in all of us. Now I'm no mind reader, but I imagine the kids in my class visualizing the ever so tasty JELL-O Dirt Cups dancing in their *heads like sugarplums the night before Christmas.*

My brothers and I just began drooling upon hearing the words *JELL-O Dirt Cups.* The three of us really loved dirt cups. It was one of our favorite treats, so we were most definitely going to remember our verses for next Sunday, but what in the world could Mrs. Paraclete be up to? She had to be up to something. Like I said, she never told us the actual *treat* we'd get.

O, please forgive me. I forgot to mention my name and my brothers' name, too. My name is **Joshua**, 12 years old. I am the big brother. I'm also known as "Bible boy" by my youngest brother. For any situation, I've been told that I can find a Bible verse for it. Next in line after me is **Saul**, 11 years old—a.k.a. "the pray before you play kid." Ask him to play anything, and before you knew it, you'd be in a circle of prayer faster than you can say "Duck, duck goose!" And lastly, there was **Gabriel**, 9 years old. Of course, if you ask him, he'd tell you he's 9½. We called him Gabe, or "angel of our mother," who much like the angel Gabriel in the Bible stood in the presence of God, he loved being in mom's presence—yep, you guessed it. He's a momma's boy and the youngest of the three of us.

Now I mentioned before that I am no mind reader, but Mrs. Paraclete must be an exception to *that* rule. For no sooner I began to envision our whole class scarfing down JELL-O Dirt Cups, she spoke these words to us, **"Do not remember your Bible memory verse for a treat, but treat someone with your memory verse– for it is the greatest treat to the heart."**

I, then, looked around our classroom, and much like everyone else, I wasn't the only one confused by her words. Someone in the class even had the *nerve* to try and repeat what she said, "Treat your verse to dinner?" And needless to say, the entire class exploded in laughter. "Never mind," she said holding back her giggled grin. "Just know your verses for next week."

So like every Sunday, as we are leaving out of the classroom, she handed us our assigned memory verses—*with a smile*. She gave me John 3:16; to Saul she gave Romans 5:8 and Gabe was given Matthew 16:18.

After getting our verses, my brothers and I—as we always did—thoughtlessly shoved them in our back pockets. We always forgot we put them back there and the only way we remembered we had put them back there was when our mom was doing laundry. Then she'd call us down to retrieve our verses. We were supposed to put them in this crystal see-through container our parents called *The Hiding Place.*

The Hiding Place container was placed at the center of the dining room table in our house with some words engraved around it. I don't know what the words on it said, but it's very pretty. It's a crystal-shaped heart surrounded with smooth pebbles. It gave the dining room a really serene and peaceful feel to it. Truthfully, though, I don't know why they called it the *hiding* place when it was in plain sight every night at dinner.

So anyway, after mom's relay message to our dad about our memory verses, he would give us our weekly lecture after we forgot our verses in our back pockets - *again*. He'd always say, "**We are creatures of forgetfulness, but memory is a skill. So choose to _not_ forget**." We never questioned our dad when he gave us words of wisdom. We just nodded our heads in silent agreement and moved out of his presence as fast as we could so he couldn't come up with more wise, but confusing, words to say. I mean, it was enough that we had to memorize our Bible verses for "crying out loud."

WELL, MY BROTHERS AND I only lived a few blocks away from the church. And after much begging over the years, our parents let us walk home by ourselves every Sunday. My parents told me I was pretty mature for my age. So I take it this is why they let us walk home alone, or maybe it was the fact I've only been begging them since I was 10 years old.

One day I begged them so intensely that I promised to do the unthinkable. No kid in their right mind ever promises to do what I'm about to say. I promised my parents that if they let us walk home alone from church every Sunday, I'd stop playing video games for an entire week—one whole week. I know—I must be crazy, but they agreed. It was a big struggle for me, but I did it. Ever since that day, we've been walking home alone every Sunday.

Well, despite the freedom to go home by ourselves, today was not that day. Today, our parents were coming with us.

I know it's Halloween Day on Sunday, but we do not even celebrate it, so I know we're not going trick or treating. So we all thought this was a little strange, considering two things: 1) as I just said, we usually walked home alone every Sunday and 2) Mrs. Paraclete's revealing of our treat for next Sunday.

Saul, then, spoke up and asked them, "How come you're coming with us? Are you walking us home today because…"

And then our dad, almost immediately answering him in perfect time, as if one person were speaking, finished his question, "…we're going to help you with your Bible memory verses? Why yes! That's exactly what we're going to do. Your church teacher, Mrs. Paraclete, actually called us up last week and asked if your mom and I could help you out a little bit. I mean, if that's okay with you?"

Okay with us? Of course it's okay! A little help from our parents meant fun, fun and more fun. Having our parents help out with any project or assignment of any kind always made it way more fun. Last year we had a Christmas project due in school, and they made up a Jeopardy game to teach us all the important stuff about Christmas. We used fruit roll-ups for money for every right answer—or I should say *right question.* Another time I had math homework doing fractions, and to make me understand it better, mom ordered a pizza—well, they let me order it myself. They sliced up the pizza, I learned, and o boy, did we eat! Fun stuff, I tell you.

Come to think of it, this is probably one of the reasons why Mrs. Paraclete asked our parents to help us out. We never tired of telling her the countless stories our parents did helping us with our different assignments.

Now as we are walking along, my brothers and I realize we are not walking toward our house. Now I mentioned before that we only lived a few blocks away from the church—but I didn't mention it only takes 5 minutes to get home. We get out of church at 2:00pm. So by 2:05 or 2:06, we're normally home.

Well, we've been walking for about 15 minutes in the opposite direction of our house. To make it worse, it looked like it was going to rain. It was very cloudy outside and the sun never popped out all morning. Then all of a sudden, our dad stopped dead in his tracks like *he* now realized we weren't going home—like we were going the wrong way; *we were* going the wrong way, or...***were we***?

CHAPTER 2

THE HOUSE?

Dad began to stoop down to tie his shoes, and as he was squatting down, asked us, "Do you see that **house** across the street?" We looked over there to see the house and no sooner our eyes met this house, the very hairs on our necks stood up instantly. This house definitely wasn't our home—that's for sure. We weakly responded to our dad, "Yes."

You know the expression that says *don't let your imagination run away with you?* Let's just say I should've told it to stay home because my mind started to project the craziest of thoughts—like zombies coming up out of the ground, and then being chased by a masked figure with a machete.

Wishing we'd never seen this place and regrettably thinking he might actually send us in there, yet at the same time, we hoped he wouldn't. I even overheard Saul praying under his breath. "Though I walk through the valley of the shadow of death…" Now hearing that portion of his prayer—shadow of death—sure wasn't comforting. Gabe even tried to give the pitiful puppy-dog look to our dad, but I don't think it was working too well.

Now as for this house, it was completely black. The front door was black; even the steps were black. This was a dark place, period. It was as if someone took jet-black paint and threw it over every stone of the house. And on top of the darkness, fog was everywhere—and boy, was *it* thick.

The house resembled a castle with stone walls as big as cars. The house had a very pointy triangular roof made with more stone. There wasn't even a porch light, and to make it worse, the house was massive.

The chimney up above seemed to breathe red misty smoke and it joined the surrounding fog, giving the house a bit of a red glow. Now the weirder part about this big house is that the red mist *puffed* and *breathed* in steady rhythms from the chimney like a heartbeat. The house appeared to be alive yet lifeless because of how dark it was. It felt as if we were in a scary horror movie. If the sunlight were out, it would have never even touched the ground. It was just downright dark. Not only were the hairs on our necks standing up, the ones in our noses stood up, too. And God only knows what was going through the minds of my brothers as they took sight of this dreadful house.

Then our dad looked back at us; then at our mom with a grin and then back at us again. Then he said, "This is how we are going to help you remember your Bible memory verses. And yes," he continued calmly yet enthusiastically, "it is *your job* to go…into…that…house…in order for us to help you.

All of us just blankly stared at him in shock and unbelief. Yep, they've lost it, I thought. Somewhere between breakfast this morning and church service, they must've got *fun* confused with *fear*. Isn't that what Halloween is all about? I thought we didn't celebrate Halloween. I thought we did fun without the fear. Going in this house couldn't possibly be fun! They couldn't be serious…could they? I mean, this would go against everything we believed and knew about our parents—the ones that, whenever we had some work to do, always had a way of making it fun, not scary. "But just before you go," dad continued, "let me tell you a little about this house."

My goodness, I thought. I was already on edge about going into this house. Not only is the house scary-looking, but it also has a history—and from the way our dad sounds, it has a "haunted history." Dad said, "It's been rumored that this house was built over a cemetery where they filmed the movie *Night of the Living Dead*." And my brothers and I had many nightmares about that movie every time we watched it. Needless to say, my heart was starting to skip beats for being scared and to make things worse; my hand was starting to lose sensation. I couldn't feel it—not because I was afraid, but because *Gabe* was afraid. He was standing next to me the whole time dad was talking. He was squeezing the life out my hand, and for a moment there, I couldn't get loose. I shook. I rattled… nothing. So I did the best next thing. I just put my arm around him and held him close. Hey, if you can't beat 'em, join 'em, right?

Then our dad went on to say, "This house needs **light**."

No kidding, I thought. It needs a *whole* bunch of light.

He continued, "Think of it as the '*light of life* rescue mission.' Now when you get in the house, you won't see much of anything. Upon reaching the steps leading to the front entrance, you'll find a backpack with some important stuff inside. The stuff inside the backpack will help you get through the house and give it the light it needs."

"Now you are looking for a **black cauldron**," Dad continued. "All this fog you see, it is all coming from this black cauldron you have to find."

Our dad then looked to his right, and then to his left… very slowly and cautiously, might I add.

He moved closer to us and whispered, "Now I have to warn you, the darkness is the least of your worries. Your backpack is a major threat to this house. There are terrible things in this house that will try to stop you from finding the black cauldron. These terrible things will try to take the backpack off of you, and everything in it." We looked at each other wondering what could possibly be in the bag that could be such a threat and what these *terrible things* were actually.

"Yes," he continued, "you have enemies, but don't worry. Your flashlights, one of the items inside the backpack, are a sure weapon to defeat them. Darkness cannot stand light," he said emphatically.

Still, we blankly stared at our dad in unbelief. We looked to our mom to jump in any minute and say something like, "O, alright boys, we're just kidding around with you," but she never did. Were they really for real? Are they asking us to step foot into a place that looks like a black hole, trapping forever anything that comes inside?

"Dad," I asked weakly. "Isn't there any other way?"

We all looked at him hoping he'd say yes.

"Of course, son. You always have a choice."

Our eyes started to dance with joy. Maybe we wouldn't have to go in this house after all.

"The other way to do this," our dad replied, "is to rent a helicopter, tie ropes around your waists and lower you down through the chimney."

Our eyes stopped dancing. Sarcasm, I thought. He's still making us go in the house.

"Listen guys," dad continued, "trust me and don't be scared. You have everything you need for this task. You'll be fine."

"Unfortunately," Dad said reluctantly, "we cannot go with you, but your mom and I have picked someone to lead you through the house."

Yes, our emotions were going in every direction—sad, scared, and happy, etc. Although, after hearing him say someone would be leading us through the house, we were super happy! Yet we asked among ourselves who would be the one to lead us. There were only five of us.

"Mrs. Paraclete is coming with us!" Gabe shouted out. Not a bad guess, I thought. I mean, she *did* seem to be the mastermind behind all of this, but mom shook her head no. If it wasn't Mrs. Paraclete, who could it be?

Saul asked hastily, "Well who?"

Dad extended his arms to us and said, "The leader is among you." Funny…instantly I knew…I knew whom my dad was talking about, and it really became clear to me when all eight eyes zoomed in on…me. I can't even begin to explain the fear I felt to lead my brothers through this scary-looking house. Yet, despite the fear, strangely, I felt it a real privilege. Why, though? I asked myself. Isn't it crazy to think like this? I know it was crazy to give up video games for a week, but this was different. Shouldn't I want to run away? Despite all rhyme and reason *NOT TO GO*, I feel compelled *to go*.

It seemed to be the moment of truth—the moment I've been waiting for since about the age of 10.

Well, despite the urge to lead my brothers through this house, I was still looking for a way out of this—for all of us, to just have a normal Sunday afternoon. I started to think of some excuses so we wouldn't have to go in. Then it hit me—my age! Yeah, I thought. I'm too young. All of us were! Now I usually volunteer to lead or be in charge of most things, but it was different this time. Please understand that this house looked *really really* scary. Desiring to be "grown," as mom and dad said I always tried to be at times, I chose to shrink back to being a little child—to be irresponsible... for the moment. Hopefully, dad would forget this whole assignment if we could give him a good enough reason for us not to go. So I gave my dad the most rational explanation I could give.

"We're too young!" I exclaimed in a high squeaky voice.

"Too young?" Dad asked with a big smile and chuckling softly.

"Yeah," I said further making my point. "Besides, Gabe's only 9 years old." Dad was still laughing.

"Nine and a half," Gabe corrected me quickly.

"Okay, nine and a half. The point being... we're all too young," I reasoned.

Saul lightly but firmly popped Gabe on the back of

his head with the palm of his hand as discreetly as possible without our parents noticing it. Gabe, grabbing the back of his head, quickly turned his head in Saul's direction with intense disgust.

Gritting and whispering through his teeth, Saul said to Gabe, "Shhh...unless you want to actually go in this house."

We all looked at each other nodding our heads in agreement and then peered back at our Dad for confirmation—to let us off the hook.

Dad extended his arms to us again, gently grabbed my shoulders, looked me square in my eyes and said, "But not too young to walk your brothers home from church. You're not too young to pick up the phone and order a pizza, and definitely not too young to memorize your Bible memory verses. In a nutshell, all we are asking you to do is memorize your verses."

Now as dad was talking to us, Gabe, thank God, had released his death grip from my hand. He must've became comforted by our mom's smiling face. She'd been smiling the whole time. Gabe began nudging me and said to me, "Let's just get in there...he's not letting us off the hook, and besides, the more we think about *not* going, the more we *won't* want to go at all."

"He's right, Josh," Saul agreed. "Let's do it." Dad, then, put his arm around mom's waist. Both of them were overjoyed with us accepting this task. At this point, Saul and Gabe had persuaded me to go in the house. Gabe, especially, blew me away with his compelling remark. He had spoken like one of true wisdom. I was impressed - too impressed to be scared... at least for the moment.

"Okay," I said to my dad finally accepting this mission,

"one more question." Dad nodded his head permitting me to ask.

"What else is in the bag?"

"Here," he said. "Let's go over there and take a look, shall we?"

Well, going over there meant getting closer to the house. And we were in no hurry getting there. Besides, it was twice as foggy near the house. So we just followed their lead. Dad, then, knelt beside the backpack and unzipped it. He pulled out...

"Hey! That's **mom's mirror**!" Gabe exclaimed, "I'd recognize it anywhere."

Dad handed it to Saul to hold as he grabbed the other stuff in the backpack. Now hold up just a second, I thought. Didn't dad say the things in this bag were (and I quote) "a major threat" to this house. Was he joking? How could a mirror, especially mom's pink girly mirror, threaten anything except the three of us caught walking around with it? If any of the guys in school saw us, we'd never hear the end of it. We'd be the laughing stock of all time.

"Here you go, mom," Saul said handing mom her mirror. And after having the mirror in his hand extended toward mom longer than he expected, he looked at her and wondered why she hadn't taken it. He, then, took a snapshot look at mom and dad, but mom's grin must've told him something because *then* he said in a sour tone, "O you can't be serious. A mirror? What kind of weapon is this?"

Mom replied, "The kind you need."

Well, the confusion that had visited us just a while ago had made its second appearance. Then all the other things he pulled out the bag weren't getting any better. He pulled out three **flashlights**, a **map**, remote control and three metal hearts. These weren't weapons. These were household items!

"What are we supposed to do to this house," Saul exclaimed, throwing up his arms with one of the metal hearts in one hand, "*love it to death!*" Dad smiled like Saul had said the right answer.

The only things in the backpack that actually resembled any kind of weapon were the flashlights. The handle part of them looked like sword handles off of the movie *Star Wars*. The swords in the movie were made of light, and they used them to fight. I mean, great movie and all, but sword fighting was a skill none of us had. Yeah, we playfully sword fought in our rooms, but in real life, I'm sure we suck. However, I'm sure, given these flashlights in the backpack are exactly like the swords in *Star Wars*, we could definitely learn how to sword fight the moment we enter the house. For some strange reason, though, I get the feeling these flashlights are just flashlights—and nothing more than… well, you know…flashlights.

"You don't even have to ask," dad said. "I can see the confused look on your faces. I'll explain it one more time."

Yeah, based on Saul's reaction to mom's mirror and our idea of weapons being baseball bats instead of flashlights and a map, an explanation was well in order. Maybe a stake for Count Dracula and some silver bullets for any potential werewolves would be nice. *Okay*, maybe these old scary figures (Vampires and Werewolves) don't really exist, but some real weapons would give us a little more confidence, don't you think?

"Pay close attention," dad began to explain, "to two of these items in the backpack." He picked up one of the items, which were the metal hearts. These were about as big as my hand. "These metal hearts are ***charitable explosives***. What they do is burst out a tremendous amount of really bright light upon detonation," dad motioned with his hands in big circular motions.

"Detonation," Saul exclaimed perking up. "Now that sounds like a weapon of mass destruction!"

"More than you know," dad replied. Of course, I think we all perked up when he said 'detonation.'

"In order for it to explode," dad continued, "you have to know the memory verse Mrs. Paraclete gave you today. Now here is what you do. You take one of these charitable explosives, lay the flat side of it on the wall, push the little button to turn it on—make sure it's green and not red, and…Walla…speak your memory verse. When you do this, it will latch itself onto whatever you put it on.

"What about the det…det…" Gabe stuttered.

"Detonation," Saul helped him say it.

"Yeah, detonation. When does it explode, dad?"

Dad held up the remote control. "I was just getting to that, son."

"After you have the charitable explosive on the wall, this detonates the explosive. This is called a ***3C detonator***. See the three buttons, here," he pointed them out, "and how they are numbered 1, 2, 3? Each *charitable explosive* is numbered 1, 2 or 3. The number you hit on the 3C detonator will determine what explosive is detonated. Before you go, I'll program your verses into each charitable explosive, okay?

"Okay, dad," I said, "what are the mirror and map for?" Dad answered, "I'm afraid I can't tell you, my boy, but the map will let you know everything else you need to know."

"But wait a minute, dad. I don't get it," Saul said curiously. "You said this house *needs light,* and then you said the darkness cannot *stand light.* If this is true, why does a place that needs light not...want it?"

Gabe also chimed in his question, "Yeah, and what is the light from the bombs supposed to do? Is it a weapon, too?"

At this point, mom and dad just stared at us just as blankly as we had stared at them when they told us we had to go into this house. I think they were done talking to us and answering questions. They walked toward us, and gently embraced us. Mom kissed us softly on our cheeks and looked at all of us and said, "No more questions. We have to go and so do you."

"Yeah," dad agreed. "You *do* have to go, but one last thing." He, then, reached into his pocket and pulled out a small black velvety pouch bag. "When you reach the black cauldron, you'll need this. Hold on tight to it," he urged us.

He took my hand, and placed the small black pouch in it. No doubt, being the designated leader, I guess *I* was responsible for this **little black pouch**. It felt like rocks in the pouch, but I couldn't say for sure. The pouch was all tied up, and the fact mom and dad weren't answering any more of our questions, made me a little hesitant to ask what was in it. He probably wouldn't tell me if I *did* ask, so I didn't even bother.

IN OUR FINAL PREPARATION, DAD took us aside and programmed our verses into the charitable explosives. We had to read off our memory verses into the explosives. We read it straight out Dad's Bible. When he pushed the button on the charitable explosives, it recorded us saying our verses. I guess we have to know our verses in order for it to explode when the time comes. Dad said we have to say our verses the way they're programmed in the bomb. After we were done doing that, Saul picked up the backpack with all those important items inside that dad just told us about. Our mom took our Bibles so we couldn't use them when the time came to cite our verses. I guess so considering we were supposed to remember our verses.

As we moved closer to the house and more further away from our parents, our dad made another comment. He said, "O by the way, that DO NOT ENTER sign posted up above the door…it's old. Don't pay it any mind."

Funny, we hadn't even noticed the sign until he pointed it out. Plus, the fog around us made it hard to see.

Gabe nudged me again, and expecting some more wise words from him, he said, "Where's Saul?"

He sounded a little panicky, but I responded in a matter of fact manner, "He's right here."

However, to my surprise, he wasn't standing where I thought he was standing. We looked to the right… nothing…we looked to the left…nothing. O my gosh! Had the house sucked him up right under our noses without us even knowing about it? Where was he? I took a step back and –

"UGGH!"

"What was that?!" Gabe exclaimed. Mom and dad turned around to see what all the fuss was about. Finally we looked down where the noise was coming from, and lo and behold, there was Saul on the ground.

"Ool, I'm sorry Saul," I said in a relieved tone of voice. We thought we'd lost him. "Are you okay?" I continued.

"I'd be worse if you were 10 lbs. heavier… But yes, I'm fine," Saul said jokingly.

Gabe was still panicked and outraged, and asked indignantly, "WHAT WERE YOU TRYING TO DO— SCARE US HALF TO DEATH!"

"No," Saul replied calmly because Gabe was all worked up, "I was on the ground praying."

"Lying on your face, Saul," Gabe answered back like he had sour gum in his mouth.

"Yeah," Saul calmly continued on. "It was customary in Bible days to lay prostrate on the ground and pray."

"Well," Gabe continued, "can you give us a warning… you know… the next time you decide to lie p-pro… prostr…"

"Prostrate," Saul helped him as he stuttered over the word.

"*Whatever*," Gabe said.

Mom started to chuckle a little bit. Dad did too. "You kids are hilarious," dad said. So after helping Saul to his feet, he picked up the backpack and we were on our way to a most dreadful place. Now it was time for business.

Still chuckling, mom pulled out a piece of paper out of her Bible. Dad motioned to us to listen as she began to read. Very calmly, as always, (and I guess this is where Saul got his serene nature—from mom) mom began to read aloud.

"*'Haven't I commanded you? Strength! Courage! Don't be afraid; don't get discouraged. God, your God, is with you every step you take. Joshua chapter one verse nine.*"

"To keep from being afraid," mom continued, "**respect**

God and His power, **respect the power of fear** and when you reach the cauldron, **respect the power of sin**. The ***three fears of faith*** will get you through this house."

With that, she folded the paper back up and put it in her Bible. The words sunk deep in my heart. We were hushed like 'a calm' before the storm. We could have heard a pin drop all the way on the moon.

Our parents gave us one final wave, and within seconds, were out of sight. Now it's just *us* …and… the *house*.

CHAPTER 3

THE FACELESS ENCOUNTER

Now it is just the three of us. Our parents are gone, and we are preparing ourselves to go into the house.

"We'd better get in there," Saul said. And being the professional prayerologist he was, he advised that we pray before heading in this house.

"Gabe?" Saul called teasing him. "We're about to prostrate ourselves in prayer. Are you ready?"

"You think you're pretty funny, don't you prayer boy?" Gabe chuckled back. "Well, I just wanted to cover myself this time," Saul replied.

"Alright guys, let's pray already," I interrupted.

So we bent down on one knee together (lying down on the ground seemed just a little extreme), held hands in a circle and closed our eyes (well, I prayed with one eye closed and one eye open. You know...can't be too careful these days).

Saul prayed, "Father forgive our parents; for they know

not what they do, and please help us find the black pot. In Jesus' name, Amen."

"Amen? Did you say 'Amen?'" Gabe asked surprised and seemingly unsatisfied with the prayer.

"Yeah, you know…Amen…like you say at the end of a prayer," Saul answered sarcastically.

Gabe answered back, "I know what 'Amen' means prayer boy, but don't you think that prayer was a tad bit short? What about the Lord's Prayer…you know… "deliver us from evil?"

"You know, he's right Saul. You did forget something," I said sensing Gabe's fear and reluctance to go in the house. "You forgot to pray that part of the Lord 's Prayer that says… hmm…what was it again? 'Lead us not into temptation…' *to run home to mommy and daddy*," I said looking straight at Gabe.

I think Gabe got the message. "Okay, I won't run," Gabe said. He looked up toward the sky and very quickly prayed, *"And deliver us from evil.* Amen…Okay let's go."

After the prayer…or should I say…prayers…we rose to our feet. As we further approached the house, going up the steps, the fog seemed to be getting thicker, making it even harder to see than before. However, it seemed at the moment, the fog had a mind of its own. Like a big red theater curtain on stage, the fog seemed to slowly move out of our way.

Upon reaching the last step away from the porch, we noticed the porch wasn't very sturdy. It seemed it would break into pieces with the slightest bit of wind passing by it. Still, we had to check and see if it was okay to stand on.

"Anyone want to check to see if this porch can hold our weight?" I asked them.

They both acted as if they didn't hear me.

"Looks like my wristwatch isn't working," Saul said tapping his *bare* wrist.

I don't know who he thought he was fooling. Anyway, I looked over in Gabe's direction on the other side of me, and he just gazed up in the sky like he could really see anything in all this fog and darkness. So with no way to persuade them to check out the porch, I decided to check it myself.

"Fine," I said indignantly, "I guess I'll check it out myself." My imagination, once again, went crazy. Each inch closer my foot came to the unsteady looking porch, a bead of sweat popped off my forehead. My heartbeat beat like a drummer boy preparing the troops for war. Faster and faster my heart beat...my foot touched the porch...nothing. It didn't crumble beneath me. "The coast is clear, guys," I told them. Speculatively, they looked at each other for a moment, but then they stepped on with me.

CRACK... CRUMBLE... AHHHHHHHHHHHHH! SPLASH!! We'd landed in a puddle of water. We were soaked...but not too soaked.

"I thought you said the coast was clear," Gabe asked rubbing his behind to ease his pain as he made his way back to his feet.

"I'm sorry. I miscalculated. I guess it wasn't until you guys stepped on with me. All of our weight together must've been too much for it."

Now where we were looked like a back alley way at night and there was bit of a cold draft, too. We got up and wrung out the little bit of water our shirts absorbed. "Y'all okay?" I asked.

"Yeah," Saul replied, "just a little wet."

Before we fell through the porch steps, it was dark, but now it was even darker down here. "We're going to need our flashlights. I can't even see my own hand in front of my face," I said.

"I'm on it," Saul said pulling out the flashlights from the backpack…after struggling to find it, of course. After we had our flashlights in hand, we turned them on and started scanning the area. We just saw wet brick walls and water dripping from up above.

When we had fallen through the porch, we fell through a slope-like, windy zig-zaggy slide at a park. It was too slick to get back up to the top, and there wasn't any grip whatsoever to even pull ourselves up. Reaching the conclusion we couldn't get back up the way we came in, we decided to just figure out another way in the house.

"Does anyone see a way in here?" I said looking frantically.

"Here Josh, I see a door right here," Gabe pointed out to us. When we all saw the door, we noticed how black and creepy-looking it was. So creepy-looking and black this door was, that none of us dare not even so much as touch the doorknob.

In an indignant voice, Saul said, "*The only way I step foot through that door is if…*"

All of a sudden, as Saul was talking, the door had opened by itself. There was no movement from any of us—just complete silence. You could've heard another pin drop all the way on the moon.

Then Gabe finished Saul's sentence with his eyes opened wide, "…*it opens by itself.*"

"It's probably just the wind," I said trying to ease our

minds. "There *is* bit of a draft down here." Saul, then, grabbed the map from the backpack. Come to think of it, we hadn't even had a chance to look at the map before we fell through the unsteady porch. I wondered if being down here in this dungeon-like place put us somewhere the map *wouldn't* show.

"What does the map say?" I asked him hoping the map could pinpoint our location.

"Well," he answered as he continued reading the map, "it says –"

"Hey," Gabe interrupted, "Look at this metal thing on the ground."

"What is it?" I asked.

"(Ahem)…excuse me," Saul chimed in clearing his voice. "I believe I was asked a question. May I answer it please?" We had got so caught up with the new discovery on the ground, I'd forgotten I asked him a question.

"Well," Saul continued, "the map says that there should be a plaque at the front entrance of the house with an engraved message on it."

"We are no longer at the front entrance," Gabe added, "I guess we just skip that part of the map."

"Wait a minute," I edged in. "Gabe, didn't you just say you saw a metal thing on the ground?" He shook his head agreeing with me. "Maybe the metal thing you saw is the plaque the map is referring to?"

"Maybe," Saul agreed. "Let's take a look and see if this *is* the plaque."

Curiously, Gabe asked, "How did it get down here? Shouldn't it be above us?"

"Maybe it fell down here with us through the porch,"

Saul replied. "Maybe it was already down here. Who knows?"

We all knelt down for a closer look. The closer we got to the metal we noticed a lot of dust on it. It resembled a plaque, but we didn't see any words on it. I, then, blew all the dust off and wiped off the rest with my hand. There was so much dust in the air after blowing and wiping it off, we all started fanning it away frantically and coughing. Then it all started to make sense. The metal plate on the ground - that was also embedded in the ground - turned out to be the plaque Saul read from the map. We were where we needed to be. We saw the inscribed message on it, too. Saul volunteered to read it.

"Hey guys, shine your flashlights on it so I can read it." So Gabe and I shined our lights on the engraved plaque and Saul began to read.

> **"LIGHT? It is not welcome here. You are only welcome if you've come to join the darkness. I am unbeatable. If you've come with your light to fight, I hope also, in your bag, you've brought your pajamas to spend the night. Fighting me will only tire you to defeat and slumber. And you—YES YOU—I will certainly plunder. Who am I? Only your worst nightmare. Enter if you dare.**
> **-Emperor Hamartia Diablo**

"**Emperor Hamartia Diablo**?" Saul repeated the name again. "I've heard of some crazy fancy names for emperors, but I've never heard of this ruler before. I wonder who he *or* she is?"

"Well it sounds like he or she really hates light," Gabe blurted out. 'Guess we better not go in here. Plus, we've got no sleeping bags."

"Good idea, Gabe. You stay here…and we'll go inside." Gabe's eyes got big again. You would've thought he'd seen a ghost or something. It was as if his heart sunk to his feet. "But if you change your mind," I continued, "you are more than welcome to join us."

Gabe started to look around the area and I guess he began to think of what it would be like to be alone down in this dark pit-like place.

"On second thought," he said chuckling with fear, "I did say earlier that the m-m-more we think about it, the more likely we won't go in, right?"

"Yeah, that's what I remembering you saying," Saul said with a smirk.

"You know Gabe…the Bible says a 'double-minded man (or boy in your case) is unstable in all his ways," I said pointing at his head as I spoke and giggled.

"Riiiggghhht," he replied dragging it out with a shaky, crackling voice. "Listen, let's save the Bible verses for the love bombs, okay Bible boy?"

Anyway, all jokes aside, now was the moment to step through this black creepy door. Saul looked at the map again for further instructions. The map told us to travel a long hallway after coming through the door, stop into some room off to the side, and then head into the kitchen. The kitchen, it said, had a secret passageway leading to what looked to be the basement. *"Basement?"* I thought to myself. Yeah, that can't possibly be good.

THE WIND PICKED UP SPEED and gusto. We'd gone through the creepy door and then the door slammed behind us. **WHAM!** We all quickly turned back toward the door to open it back up. We yanked with all our might…nothing. We were locked in.

"Great," Gabe sighed. "Could things get any worse?" No sooner he spoke Gabe let out a gasping jolt and ran into me and clung on to me—you know…his super tight death grip around my neck with his arms.

"What are you doing?" I whispered loudly trying to catch my breath.

"There was something breathing on my leg!" he responded faintly and weakly. "Hey, hold up a sec. Where's Saul?" I said figuring it was Saul breathing on Gabe's leg.

"Sorry guys, I was praying again," Saul said. We shined our lights toward the direction we heard Saul's voice. He was on the floor…*again*. We just shined our flashlights in his face staring a hole *right* through him.

"I got scared," he pleaded as he got up off the floor.

We continued on. We aimed our flashlights down the long hallway, but our light just got lost in the darkness. The hallway was longer than we thought.

"This is the hall that doesn't end. It just goes on and on," Gabe said hopelessly. "Maybe we *should* go back this time. This hallway could go on for miles, you know."

"How?" I snapped slightly. "None of us have super powers to bust through doors, do we? Do we have wings to fly? If we're going to get out of here, we have to keep going, no matter how long the hallway is."

Snap…crackle…and pop. These sounds kept echoing through the house as we walked along. We did our best to keep silent but that would have been impossible due to the fact there were so many twigs on the floor. It was so quiet in the house. We even tried to tiptoe; still the twig snapping and noise continued.

"Someone or some*thing* is going to hear us," Saul whispered. Then an unusual noise sounded in my ear.

"Shhhh…don't move," I cautioned. Neither of them moved. "What was that?" I spoke softly with bit of a startle.

"See, I told you we should've gone back," Gabe panicked.

I snapped again, "Gabe, didn't I just tell you…"

CREEEK. I heard it again. "It sounds like footsteps, and they're getting closer, you guys," Saul confirmed. Yeah, I'll admit, my heart was in my throat now.

We all shined our flashlights in the direction we heard the footsteps. And just as soon as we nailed down the direction they were coming from, they stopped. Silence…again. All we heard now was our own breathing, and as ridiculous as this may sound, I could even hear us blinking. Yes, it was *that* quiet. We dashed our lights around the hallway looking for the one responsible for those footsteps.

The fog that had left us as we neared the house before falling through the porch was coming back. As the red misty fog returned, we heard something else. This time it wasn't the sound of footsteps; it was the sound of a door opening—opening very slowly. Then the footsteps began to sound off again. Now they were coming toward us. They were getting louder with each step.

"There's nowhere to hide," I whispered. "It's nothing but walls around us." "Quick," Saul motioned, "turn off your flashlights."

Reluctant to turn off his flashlight, Gabe said, "But didn't dad say…"

"JUST DO IT GABE!" Saul and I shouted softly.

The lights were out. We were all hunched together squatting down on the floor, hoping not to be seen. It was also super dark because we'd just turned off our flashlights. Our eyes didn't have enough time to adjust to the darkness, so we couldn't even see what was coming toward us. Whatever it is was or whoever it was didn't seem to be stumbling through the darkness, almost like it had lived in the house for many years or had those special binoculars to see in the dark. Gabe was shaking hard enough to start an earthquake.

The closer the sound of the footsteps got, my eyes finally started to adjust to the darkness to see a little better. I was finally able to match the footsteps with the shape of a person. The shape looked like a man. Still, it was too dark to make out what this person looked like. Suddenly this person stopped walking and looked around. I guess he didn't see us because we were right under his nose - *literally*. Its foot was only inches away from mine own.

We were dead still. We didn't move a muscle. We stayed as quiet as we could while this **black figure** looked around. Each time its foot moved I thought it was going to touch mine, and then we'd be dead for sure. No sooner this black figure walked toward us, though, it was now walking away from us. It was going back in the direction it came but just as this black figure was out of sight, Gabe bumped Saul and made him drop his flashlight. The sound of my flashlight dropping echoed throughout this entire house. I looked at the black figure again. The next thing I knew, it turned around and began walking back in our direction, but a lot faster this time. I have to *do something*, I thought, as my heart raced as fast as he was coming toward us. So I did the smartest thing I could think of.

I let out a loud scream, jumped on the black figure like a monkey, hitting him over and over again.

"Get away from us! Get away from us!" I shouted. It didn't seem to be affected by any of my blows at all. Next thing I knew, it was trying to take my flashlight off of me.

I heard Saul scream out, "Josh, hold on tight! Don't let him take your flashlight!" I hollered back panting and struggling, "I'm...I'm trying! Help!"

Why isn't the flashlight working, I thought? Dad said it was a weapon, and the handle looked like a sword handle, yet every hit was like striking out in a baseball game. Little by little I felt my flashlight slipping away as this monster pulled it from me.

"HELP ME!" I screamed again.

Suddenly, a white light blinded me, and I heard a loud holler, big and deep, bellow throughout the house. Very quickly, I regained my flashlight back effortlessly. The black monster had let go. Then I finally saw this black figure, with Gabe's light all over him, and a green glimmer bouncing off of this black figure, but soon discovered something more frightening. Even in the light, the black figure was *still* black, and worst of all, **he had no face**! We all screamed and ran for the door we entered through. However, as we were running, the black figure was running scared, too. Saul and Gabe kept running, but I stopped.

I looked down at the flashlight in my hand…then looked back up at the black figure running away from us. Now was he running from us, *or* the flashlight? I thought.

"Help…help…get us out of here!" Gabe and Saul yelled out yanking on the door and banging on it.

"Guys," I shouted softly. For all the loud screaming and door banging, they couldn't hear me. So I tried again, but I shouted a little louder this time.

"Guys!" Nothing. They kept banging and yelling. This time I cupped my mouth with both hands and shouted with all of my might.

"GUYS!!!" They finally stopped and turned toward me as I shined the flashlight on the both of them.

"He's gone." I assured them. "I think *we* scared him off."

"Who *was* that guy or what was that?" Gabe asked frightened and catching his breath.

"I think it was one of those *terrible things* dad said was in here. It even tried to take Josh's flashlight." Saul responded back.

"Yeah," I agreed, "and it was super strong, but after Gabe shined his flashlight on it, it ran away."

"I guess that explains why this dark house can't… stand…light. **That's it**!" Saul concluded. "When Gabe shined his light on it, it ran away because it couldn't stand the light."

"Yeah," I agreed partially, "but what about the house *needing* the light? It sounds like *we need* the light for our *own* protection."

"I'm not sure big bro.," Saul replied, "but I know for sure these flashlights really *are* weapons." Gabe seemed relieved that the flashlights actually *were* weapons and I was pretty satisfied with Saul's answer, too.

"You know…when I had the light on it, it had jealousy on its chest," Gabe added.

"Gabe," I asked, "how would you be able to tell that black figure was jealous? It had no face, remember?"

"No," Gabe replied. "The word 'Jealousy' was on its chest in green letters." Saul said he hadn't seen anything green but I told them I remembered a green flash when Gabe shined the light on it. Maybe that was it.

So we continued down this long hallway. We kept our flashlights bouncing in every direction to make sure nothing jumped on us unaware. Soon, after a few minutes of walking carefully on our tippy toes so we wouldn't make any noise, we decided to get the map out to make sure we were going the right way. Saul began to read it. Then he told us we were getting closer to our next destination. Our next destination was...*get this*...the **Perish Room**. You believe that? As if the house wasn't spooky enough. Gee, I wonder why it's called the Perish Room?

Oddly enough, between the three of us, only two of us seemed disturbed by the name of this room we had to go into. Gabe, on the other hand, seemed thrilled by the name.

He even said after Saul read the map, "Finally some sanctuary."

"Sanctuary," Saul repeated with a puzzled look on his face. "What do you mean, sanctuary?"

"Yeah," I chimed in. "What sanctuary is there in a room called *Perish*?"

In a matter of fact way, Gabe replied, "A *parish* is a safe place from anything evil. We're safe now."

Apparently Gabe had not seen the word "perish" spelled out on the map. We went on to show him the word spelled out on the map but then decided not to because, since we've been in this house, he's been completely petrified. Now he's feeling safe. We figured not to ruin the moment. Besides, I couldn't afford another one of Gabe's death grips, because then *I* wouldn't be safe.

We finally reached the Perish Room.

"Okay, we made it," Saul said with relief. "Let me take a look at the map to see the next step."

Shining our lights on it so Saul could read, the instructions for the Perish Room read like this: **A.V. on *EverWhosO* pipe Model no. CE316**.

I, then, took my flashlight and aimed it at the pipe above our heads by the wall in the back.

"Eh, I see the model number, CE316, but what does *A.V.* stand for?" I asked.

"Not sure," Saul replied. Saul began turning and twisting the map one way and the other way trying to figure out what A.V. stood for as we continued to shine our flashlights on the map so he could see.

After looking for about a minute or two, Saul put the map down and looked at me.

"3-1-6," Saul said pointing at me.

"3-1-6 what?" I said looking at him like he was crazy. "I'm not the expert reading maps—you are, remember?"

"Charitable explosive!" Gabe chimed in excitedly.

"That's it," Saul agreed. "Charitable explosive three sixteen."

"What are you guys talking about? Charitable Explosive three...OHHHHH!"

And it was like the lights in my brain finally came on. I realized that this was the time to use the "love bombs," as Gabe called them.

"Of course," I said now enlightened. "The CE stands for Charitable Explosive and the three sixteen..."

"...is your Bible memory verse from St. John 3:16," Saul finished my sentence.

Gabe continued finishing our sentence saying, "For God so loved the world that He gave His only begotten Son that whosoever... whosoever...EVERWHOSO! It's reversed, see? A.V. must stand for **Apply Verse**...apply your verse on the pipe."

"I see," I said joyfully. The joy we were experiencing now was long overdue. We'd been so scared the whole time, that there seemed there wasn't any room for joy, but now we were making some progress.

"Gentlemen," I said standing like a superhero with his cape blowing in the wind, "We are not going to perish." I, then, took the metal heart or charitable explosive and 3C Detonator out of the bag. I took my charitable explosive, held it against the EVERWHOSO pipe model no. CE316, pushed the button and began citing my memory verse assigned to me by Mrs. Paraclete and programmed by our father:

"For God so loved the world," I began citing," that whosoever believes in Him should not PERISH, but –"

WHAM! WHAM! WHAM! We turned suddenly toward the door only to see it rattling from the force something or someone was hitting. Our hearts sank with fear once again...just when we were experiencing some joy. The door didn't seem like it could take any more of the excessive pounding it was receiving. It looked as though it would cave in and break any moment.

"FINISH CITING YOUR VERSE JOSH!!!" Saul said screaming to the top of his lungs. "CITE IT...NOW!!

"OKAY!" I agreed just as loudly. "For God so loved the world that He gave His only begotten Son that whosoever believes in Him should not perish but have everlasting life. John three sixteen."

Nothing. Nothing happened. It didn't latch itself to the pipe. Instead of the green light coming on the charitable explosive indicating that it was ready to explode, the red one came on instead meaning it wasn't ready for detonation, which means I must have did something wrong, but what did I do wrong? Did I miss a word, possibly? Maybe I didn't say it loud enough. Nevertheless, the door was still taking a pounding.

And as I went on to repeat my verse, at Saul and Gabe's "loud" advice, finished citing my verse loudly, and the door that was receiving a tremendous beating finally caved in under the intense beating, but at the same time, the green light lit up on the charitable explosive, and it finally embedded itself to the pipe.

Now you would think this would have been our salvation, after the love bomb latched on to the pipe, but we still hadn't detonated it yet. Yeah, unfortunately the 3C Detonator fell after the door busted into many pieces right in our direction.

I don't think I really need to say this, but Gabe let out a really loud high-pitched scream that could have shattered glass miles away like a soprano opera singer. Saul took his hand, thank God, and covered his mouth, completely muffling his scream, eventually shutting him up.

We all looked up at the door only to see a whole bunch of black figures huddled together moving toward us slowly and discreetly. Mind you, these things are really strong. I had the time of my life just trying to get my flashlight off of one of them. They didn't speak, and what was worse, we couldn't see their eyes... for they had no eyes. So we had no way of knowing what they would do next. My brain went crazy as to what they might do to us.

And just when you thought it couldn't get any worse, it did. When the 3C detonator had dropped, it landed right in the middle of the floor, right between us and these black figures. They were by the door (or at least by the entrance way where the door once was) and our backs were up against the wall, literally.

I couldn't see their eyes, but I could tell they were ready to take the detonator, assuming before that one of them tried to take my flashlight. What were we going to do? The only way we were going to get that 3C detonator was by making a dive for it and hitting the button immediately, but would end up in the hands of these black figures that had no faces...and I think it bears repeating...***black figures that had no faces***.

In other words, someone was going to have to risk being captured in order to detonate that 3C detonator. It's the only way we were going to be saved, but who would make the dive? Who would be brave enough to detonate the detonator?

CHAPTER 4

BREWING DEATH

A hush swept through the house. All the build-up of suspense had released itself. We were still alive, thank God. I knew we were still alive because the Perish Room we were in was lit up like the Fourth of July grand finale. Not only was the room itself lit up, the entire hallway—that long hallway we'd been walking—had lit up too. We walked out of the room toward the hallway. Apparently there were pipes up above toward the ceiling of the hallway.

The unfortunate part of this great news is that the whole house was not lit up. Every part of the house we'd already been was lit up but seemingly the parts we had not been were still deathly dark.

Who had made a dive for the 3C Detonator? It was I—scared as ever, but I had to. I couldn't let those black things grab it or us. Although, those black creatures did get a hold of me as I dove for the detonator and were pulling me into the darkness, but after I hit the number one on the detonator, those lights saved my life. Just as they were dragging me closer to the darkness, they let me go. I quickly shuffled back into the light to leave them no opportunity to suck me away. It was either make a dive for it or we'd all be snuffed away into the darkness.

After getting my bearings, I looked to see if my brothers were okay. Well, my hand was turning purple again, so needless to say, Gabe was a bit shook up and Saul looked pale.

"I don't know how much more I can take of those things," Saul said with a big worried look on his face. "Every time we seem to be making any progress, here they come…" After a long pause, Saul concluded by surprisingly saying, "I just want to go home."

"I'm with Saul," Gabe agreed. "All we have to do is go back the way we came in. All the lights back there are on."

"How soon we forget. Yeah, the lights are on but you guys are forgetting about the slippery slope we fell through," I reasoned. "We can't get back out that way, remember?

My brothers were silent after what I said. Saul just kind of sat there on the floor, pitifully looking at the map. After violently yet lovingly shaking Gabe's death grip, coddling my hand for pain relief, I suggested we pray.

"For what?" Saul said still looking at the map. Then he looked up at me and said, "All the praying we've done and where's it got us?

"HERE," I said confidently. "Right here. We have followed the map pretty much to the letter. Yeah, we haven't got to the black pot yet, but we are on our way. We're closer than we were before." I was shocked at Saul's reaction to my suggestion because, as Gabe called him, he was… *the prayer boy.*

"Josh, look at this," Saul handed me the map with an aura of shock in his voice. "Dad knew we'd be scared when we got here."

"What are you talking about? Dad wouldn't intentionally..."

"Just look at the part of the map by the Perish Room," Saul interrupted me. I looked down at the map. Scanning for the Perish Room, I saw the word FEAR #1. That's weird, I thought. I repeated aloud to Saul and Gabe with a bit of doubt in my tone, "It says "FEAR #1."

"Exactly Josh. Doesn't that mean anything to you? Two more of our destinations say FEAR # 2 called **Brewing Death** and FEAR # 3 **The Gates of Hell**. You know what that tells me?"

"What?"

"Praying won't help."

"Wait a minute, wait a minute," I said. "Are you listening to yourself? Prayer won't help? Dad's methods—I agree—seem to be bit much this time, but c'mon Saul, you can't believe what you're saying." I was hoping my big brotherly tone would help him get a hold of himself. Fortunately, Saul looked as if my words had penetrated, and I am glad they did. If he would have kept making negative comments, I don't know what I would have said next.

Now there was just silence. We all knew what the next step was. We had to leave the Perish Room. I guess we had to face our next fear. The only problem is that we didn't even know what we were going to be facing, but we were terrified of it—whatever it was.

Gabe was sitting on the floor. I hadn't noticed it but he was sobbing quietly. Understanding his tears, I slowly walked toward him, knelt beside him and put my arm around him. He wiped his eyes repeatedly with his palms and his shirt, sniffling every five seconds. I continued to hold him, patting him gently. Saul was still silent.

"Listen," I affirmed strongly, "Mom and Dad told me to look out for you—the both of you—and that's what's I'm going to do. I need you guys to trust me. We have to stop being scared."

The atmosphere was starting to change, as if something I said had done it. The feeling of terror wasn't there. Saul's silence was broken.

He prayed aloud, "The Lord is my shepherd; I shall not want…"

Both of his hands were in the air. He had dropped the map on the floor, and started praying. I moved my hand from Gabe's back and slid it into his hand, grabbed it and guided him over by Saul and we joined him in prayer.

"…Though I walk through the valley of the shadow of death," we prayed along with him, "I will fear no evil. For Thy rod and Thy staff; they comfort me. Surely goodness and mercy shall follow me all the days of my life. Amen."

No sooner Saul said 'Amen,' we heard a sound coming from beneath us –a vibration. It seemed to be coming from the bag we had with us. Gabe picked it up and searched for where the sound was coming from. After rummaging through it as quickly as possible before whatever it was stopped vibrating, finally he found it and pulled it out like it was what he was looking for his whole life. As it turned out, it was a cell phone. On the screen it said "Incoming Call."

"Is there anything on the map," Gabe said perceptively, "about a cell phone?"

"No, nothing," Saul answered.

"Why didn't Dad mention that there was a phone in the bag?" I asked.

The phone continued to vibrate as we just looked at it, not knowing who would be on the other end. Finally the phone stopped vibrating.

"We'll just check the message." I said defensively.

"That's kind of silly big brother," Gabe chuckled, "it's not even our phone. Wouldn't we need a pin number? Maybe we should just answer it."

"Yeah," Saul agreed, "maybe we should just answer it… if they call a…" (Vvvvv. Vvvvv). The phone started vibrating again.

"Let's just answer it," Gabe said.

I watched Gabe's thumb move toward the TALK button, wondering whose voice would be on the other end when he pushed it. The phone lit up and was raised to his ear, opened his mouth to speak, but before his mouth could release any words, a pleasant woman's voice filled with joy and pomp began speaking.

"I see you guys are putting those verses to good use."

"MRS. PARACLETE!" we all said together with lots of excitement. We were so happy to hear a voice we recognized, especially since she could also get us out of here. But it doesn't make any since though. There's a phone in the bag Dad didn't tell us about and out of nowhere, Mrs. Paraclete just happens to call. Knowing how Dad was, he probably set this up. What are the odds she brings up "verses" which I had just used to detonate the charitable explosives? So as Gabe and Saul were excitedly talking to

Mrs. Paraclete, I quickly ended the small talk, cutting right to the chase.

"It is a pleasure hearing from you Mrs. Paraclete," I said as I took the phone away from Gabe's ear, "but…"

"You are wondering what's going on," she finished my sentence.

"Yes,"

"Well, before I say anything, put the phone on speakerphone so you all can hear me." I held the phone up and pushed the button.

"Can you hear me?" I asked loudly.

"Yes, I can hear you. Can you all hear me?"

"Loud and clear," Gabe responded.

Good. I'm sure, by now, you've figured out that you are not in a haunted house."

We were silent. If it wasn't a haunted house, what else could it be? It couldn't be a scary ride at an amusement park. We've been in here for at least an hour. No ride is that long!

"We're in a movie!" Gabe exclaimed. "This is so cool. I always wanted to be in a movie. We'll probably get an Emmy for best young actors in the 21st century!"

A chuckle came from the phone. "I wish that were true," she said laughingly.

We were all relieved at Mrs. Paraclete's response to Gabe. I was waiting for a camera crew to come from a door we hadn't seen or under the floor, like the unexpected cell phone.

"Yeah," Gabe continued, "we probably wouldn't get best actors. We probably will get a nice paycheck, though. We will –"

Mrs. Paraclete interrupted, "No, I wish it were true

that this was just a movie, but the place you stand now is definitely haunted."

All the blood in our face flushed right to our feet. None of us spoke.

"No," she assured us, "it's not haunted with ghosts and goblins—nothing like that. Keep in mind that this is not a house, though."

She continued, "Do you remember what I said to you about an hour and half ago? Do you remember what I said about 'the greatest treat'?"

"You said, 'The greatest treat is our verse to the heart,' or something like that," Saul replied.

"Exactly," she said excitedly. "You are in a *haunted heart*, not a haunted house!"

"I don't understand," Saul said puzzled. "Are we supposed to memorize our verse by heart? Does this house represent our own hearts?"

Listening for a voice to respond, instead all we heard was this: [BEEP] Sorry. The person you are trying to reach is unavailable. Please hang up and try your call again. Thank you.

I picked up the phone off the ground and went back to RECENT CALLS. I scrolled to recent calls. I pushed it to call back Mrs. Paraclete. I put the phone to my ear, but I heard no dial tone. I looked at the screen of the phone and there wasn't any light emitting from it. It had died. I tried turning it back on over and over again but it would keep shutting off.

"Great," I said in frustration. "Is there a cell phone charger inside that bag?

Saul looked diligently for about 3-4 minutes. He even

dumped the bag upside down letting all of the contents fall out onto the floor. Nothing.

"What was the point of her calling?" Gabe asked doubtingly. "She didn't give us any 'real' information. We know about as much as we did when we first fell through the porch...nothing."

Saul was sitting on the floor with the map held close to his face.

"Anything Saul?" I asked pitifully.

Saul didn't answer. He seemed to be concentrating pretty intensely. So I moved toward him to look at the map.

Saul finally answered, "Nothing. We just have to move to Destination Fear # 2, Brewing Death.

"Alright guys, let's move out," I said forcibly. "We'll never get out of here if we don't get a move on."

As we trailed the dark hallway with our flashlights, we realized this hallway resembled the other hallway we had come through—wet walls, twigs on the floor and a cold draft. The hallway was also just as long as the other one we'd come through.

About 3 minutes walking, we saw a painting hanging on the wall to our left. The painting was that of a king sitting on his throne. We analyzed it further only to find out, "This is Emperor Diablo Hamartia," Saul said in a "aha" moment.

"Emperor *who*?" Gabe said with a perplexed look on his face.

"Remember the plaque when we fell through the porch, about light not being welcome here?"

Gabe remembered and responded, "Whoa, he looks like that!?"

At the emperor's feet were what seemed to be all kinds of people sleeping and with chains around their wrists and ankles.

The emperor himself looked a little crazy. He had wild, untamed hair with reddish looking eyes and a reddish pale skin complexion. In his hand was a broken key. He looked happy and sad, if that makes any sense.

"What's with the chains? He looks more like a slave master than an emperor," Gabe commented.

As we all stared at the painting, we were suddenly engulfed by a hideous odor. It was so stinky we all pinched our noses with one hand and waving away the smell with the other. It smelled like raw eggs with a mix of elephant poop at the zoo. The smell was absolutely unbearable. I could almost imagine green misty smoke surrounding us. *I didn't even want to open my mouth.*

The smell was so bad we all took a couple of paces backward to avoid the horrible odor. After about 20 steps back, we didn't smell it as strongly any more.

"I think I'm gonna be sick."

"Me, too," I agreed with Saul.

"Where is that smell coming from?" Gabe asked pinching his nose.

"Don't know," Saul replied with the upper part of his shirt pulled over his nose to block the awful odor.

We started scanning the hallway with our flashlights, hoping to find some type of explanation for the smell. From a distance I spotted a sign. It looked antiquish, made out of wood and dusty, but was unable to make out if there were any words on it. I pointed it out to Saul and Gabe, encouraging them to walk with me toward the sign. It was toward where we initially smelled the bad odor.

It felt like we were swimming under water because breathing was out the question. I think we all took deep breaths before we walked further into the odor. As we continued to walk, I saw what looked like a kitchen. I couldn't tell for sure. We finally reached the sign I'd seen from a distance. There was writing on the sign. It read like this: **Brewing Death**.

"Brewing death?" I asked aloud talking to myself.

"Brewing what," Saul asked.

"Death. It says 'brewing death.'"

"What does that mean?" Gabe chimed in.

"Maybe that odor..." (Saul paused and looked at the map) "That's it! That bad odor is Death Brewing. That's gotta be it."

"How can you be so sure? Does the map say something about it?" I interrogated.

"As a matter of fact," Saul pointing at the map, "it does. Well...not exactly." He, then, gave me the map. He continued, "Here, look for yourself."

After scanning the map for this new discovery, Gabe brought his index finger to the exact place Saul was talking about.

"There," Gabe said.

On the spot he pointed out, there was a kitchen with a picture of a pot brewing the Grim Reaper. Surrounding the picture of the Grim Reaper and brewing pot were about 5 caskets evenly spaced out. Underneath all of this was a Scripture from 1 Peter 4:8 that said, "**ABOVE** ALL, LOVE

EACH OTHER DEEPLY, BECAUSE LOVE **COVERS OVER** A MULTITUDE OF SINS."

"Love must be the key to all of this," I concluded.

"Why do you think love is the key?" Saul asked with much interest.

At the question, I started to think about everything Mom and Dad had said and our beginning point up to now. I thought about the charitable explosives and how they gave off so much light at detonation, completely running off those black figures. I even thought of all of our memory verses Mrs. Paraclete gave to us. They were all about love. Mine was John 3:16, "God so loved the world…," Saul's was…*and then…* it hit me.

"Saul, you're next," I said excitedly.

"Next for what…death," he said with a chuckle.

I didn't say anything. I just looked at him with an affirming look. He knew. He had to know he was right. Gabe even caught on.

"Brewing Death," Gabe said with confidence "This is Fear # 2. Your memory verse, Saul. You have to speak your memory verse like Josh did in the Perish Room."

Saul stood there processing what we told him. He didn't speak for a moment.

Saul finally spoke, "So you are basically saying…"

WHAM! WHAM! WHAM!

We turned our heads quickly in the direction we heard the loud banging—directly behind us.

"That can't possibly be good," I said with reluctance in my voice. I quickly turned back to Saul putting my hand on his shoulder and said, "Love is the key because all of our memory verses are infused with love messages."

Saul went into the bag and pulled out the second charitable explosive and the 3C Detonator. He ran up the hallway with his flashlight in hand as well, encountering again the hideous odor we had so desperately retreated.

"Hurry Saul," I rushed him.

As we followed him in a rush, I noticed something up above us, but it wasn't just pipes. Something was hanging on the pipes. I saw them as we were running and my flashlight was bouncing around. As I neared these things hanging on the pipes, I slowed down to get a better view.

WHAM! WHAM!

The banging got louder. Worse, we were dealing with this foul odor. The smell really made it hard to function. As I tried to examine what was above us, I pinched my nose to keep from smelling the bad odor, but it didn't help because whenever I opened my mouth to breath I felt sick from the smell. It's like I could taste the odor.

I finally saw what was hanging above us. They were masks. Actually, they looked like gas...masks. That's it! Yes! The Scripture on the map said, "**ABOVE** ALL, LOVE EACH...,"

"Above!" I shouted. Saul and Gabe looked back at me like I was crazy. Saul had placed his charitable explosive in the kitchen doorway, citing his memory verse, but nothing was happening—no explosive light. I jumped up on the pipes and pulled them down. And there just happened to be three of them. Saul and Gabe came back over to me.

"Here, put these on," I urged them handing them the gas masks.

Once we had them on, I no longer smelled the bad odor.

In a deep voice, Saul said, "Hey I do not smell the bad odor anymore."

"Whoa," Gabe said. "You sound like Darth Vader."

"So do you."

"And so do you," Saul said to me.

We all sounded like Darth Vader with deep raspy voices and deep loud breathing, but better than anything else, we couldn't smell that hideous odor.

"How did you figure it out?" Saul inquired.

WHAM! WHAM! CRACK!

"No time to explain. Let's get out of here. To the kitchen!" I pushed them along.

As we were hurrying to the kitchen we saw caskets—some open and some closed. We stopped. Huffing and puffing I looked around for pipes with A.V. on it. We scanned the room frantically with our flashlights.

"What are we looking for?" Gabe asked looking to his left and then to his right.

"Pipes."

"Pipes?" Saul asked me with a hint of perplexity in his voice.

"Yes, pipes. Without the pipes, we will not be able to move on," I said quickly still searching for pipes in the kitchen.

"There!" exclaimed Gabe. "A pipe...over there...running through that open casket by the wall.

We rushed over there to it. We looked inside the casket with our flashlights. It was empty. Thank God, I thought. I thought a black figure would have jumped out at us but it didn't.

"But I thought we were supposed to put the charitable explosives in the kitchen doorway," said Saul. "I just thought with that painting, the bad smell and the Death Brewing sign that it wouldn't be pipes this time."

"No…like I said, it's definitely the pipes…" (*footsteps in the distance were quickly approaching*) "Speaking of pipes…" as I heard footsteps coming toward us.

"Gotcha big bro," Saul said understanding that we didn't have much time.

"There it is—'A.V. on *DeathWish* pipe Model no. CE58,'" Gabe pointed out.

Saul quickly set up to speak his memory verse into his charitable explosive. After quoting Romans 5:8, without any difficulty, his explosive latched to the pipe. He took the 3C Detonator, hit the number 2 button and…Walla—*let there be light!*

The footsteps that were getting closer to us seemed to be headed back in the direction in which they'd come. Just like before, the light scared them off back into the darkness of this…haunted heart.

"We did it!" exclaimed Gabe.

I, however, was a bit puzzled.

"What's wrong Josh?" Gabe asked me with concern in his voice.

I hadn't realized until now that there were no other doors in the kitchen, and no windows.

"Where do we go from here? There's no way out."

"Good point," Saul concurred. "I don't know."

"Well…what does the map say?" Gabe asked in a matter of fact way.

Saul went into his back pocket and pulled out the map. He had the map into many folds, so when we finally opened it up, it was super crinkly. We all huddled around Saul holding the map and began looking for the next step. We knew there was one more step to go.

We talked among ourselves, searching and throwing out many possibilities but we couldn't find anything that told us what to do next—nothing at all. With the room being well-lit, we even started to look around the room to see if we could find any clues that would tell us what to do next.

We must've spent at least a half-hour looking around the room along with a long range of ideas of what could possibly be the next step. Finally, I was starting to feel hopeless. I think my brothers were starting to feel it, too.

I guess as a response to our present situation, Gabe decided to crack a couple of jokes.

"I know you guys," Gabe said, "probably think I'm crazy for saying this but maybe we're supposed to spend the night, here!"

"And where in the world would you get an idea like that," Saul said sarcastically as he and I looked at each other with a smirk.

"Emperor Harmarshoo," Gabe said plainly.

"You mean, Emperor Hamartia," Saul corrected him.

"Whatever."

"What about him?" I asked Gabe.

"Remember what he said? We'll have to spend the night here. We can't figure this thing out. Maybe these coffins are really beds?"

I knew Gabe's words were ridiculous but at the same time, he had a point. It *was* getting later.

"Are you really considering sleeping overnight in this… *haunted*…and I put the emphasis on *haunted*…heart?" Saul asked patting his chest.

"Besides," Saul continued, "what good will it do for us to sleep here? We'll only be here longer, and I don't think any of us want that."

Now Gabe seemed to be reconsidering what he had just said, but seeing no other way to move on to the next step.

"I don't know about you guys, but I'm tired," Gabe said walking toward the casket as he stretched and yawned.

"You can't be serious," Saul said in shock. "You're lying down in the casket?"

"What do you want from me prayer boy?"

We just watched him climb into the empty casket where Saul latched his explosive on the pipe. What could we say, really? We had no answers.

The only thing I was thinking as Gabe lay in the casket was the cell phone we had. I started thinking maybe the charger might be right here in the kitchen. Without telling any of my brothers, I started looking for it. In the midst of looking, I heard a loud blood-curling scream come from the casket Gabe had lain down in.

Saul and I both ran quickly to the casket. We looked in the casket. **Gabe was gone!** All we saw was red misty smoke rising up out of the casket. Beyond that, all we saw was darkness. As we looked in the casket, it resembled a deep well. It seemed that the bottom of the casket gave as Gabe lay in it.

"This is *that* secret passageway, Josh," Saul said.

Yes, I remember him pointing it out before when we fell through the porch about two hours ago. Now, however, my focus shifted right back to Gabe.

"GABE! WHERE ARE YOU?" I shouted.

"DOWN HERE," he replied weakly and stunned.

"ARE YOU OKAY?" Saul shouted down.

"YEAH."

"We need to get him out of there," Saul said to me.

Before Saul could begin searching for something to get him out Gabe shouted up to us, "GIVE ME A FLASHLIGHT. I THINK I SEE SOMETHING!"

Saul grabbed Gabe's flashlight, looked down the hole and said, "OKAY, CATCH!"

"SEE ANYTHING LITTLE BRO.?" Saul screamed down.

There was no answer. Saul repeated himself, but still no answer.

"Why isn't he answering us," I asked.

Then I noticed something peculiar on the casket. I saw letters. I began to move my hands to get a better view. When I moved my hands completely off the casket, my heart dropped to my feet.

"What's wrong Josh? You look pale."

I just pointed to the letters I saw. Saul looked and had become just as pale as I.

CHAPTER 5

THE GATES OF HELL

The pipe to which Saul had latched his charitable explosive actually ran directly alongside the casket through the floor down to where Gabe fell. We could see *that much* with the help of our flashlights as we peered down the hole.

While we were pale at the sight of those words, 'Gates of Hell' on the casket, we were also happy at the same time because we knew we were getting closer to getting out of this God-forsaken place.

Gabe had finally answered Saul and described everything he saw even in this *lower-level* basement. He mentioned seeing a giant steel gate he could not open—an all black gate at that. *How ironic.* The pipe that ran alongside the casket through the floor also went through one of the holes of the steel black gate. I asked him if he saw any black figures, and thankfully he said no.

"Change of plans bro.," I said picking up the bag

regrettably yet cheerfully, "we're not getting him out…we're going down to him—in this hole. I believe our journey *ends…*down there."

"I guess you're right," Saul agreed. "Fear # 3, the gates of hell, is our last fear to face, but how are we going to get down there? There's nothing to break our fall."

"Good point."

"GABE!" I shouted down to him.

"YES!"

"DO YOU SEE ANYTHING DOWN THERE THAT COULD HELP US DOWN THERE?"

After a few moments of silence, Gabe found a wooden ladder and placed it so we could climb down.

"BE CAREFUL GUYS. IT FELT A LITTLE WEAK!"

"JUST HOLD IT AS STEADY AS YOU CAN, OKAY!" I shouted back.

"Saul, you first."

Saul carefully stepped up into the casket. Gabe was shining his flashlight up on the ladder to aide Saul down the ladder. Saul found his footing on the ladder and proceeded down toward Gabe. About a quarter of the way down, Saul asked me for the bag with all of our "weapons," holding the bag in one arm and keeping one arm on the ladder.

I followed along, and just as an extra precaution, closed the casket over my head to keep away any potential faceless encounters.

We now were all down in this deeper, much darker, basement, directly facing the steel black gate. It was twice as tall as we were and went all the way to the ceiling, completely blocking any way around, through or underneath it. It still reeked of the foul odor, but it wasn't as bad down here, especially since I closed the casket. So by this time, we had taken off our gas masks and put them in the bag. *Who knows? We might need them again.*

Standing in front of the gate, we started looking for a way to get through it, but there wasn't any way to get through—no way to get around, over or under it. Behind us was a great big wall with no doors or windows.

"Now what?" Gabe asked with his hands on his hips.

"Beats me. What's the map say?"

"Nothing," Saul said in disbelief. "All it says is Fear # 3: The Gates of Hell."

"What about that pipe above us," Gabe asked. "Maybe that pipe is for me?"

"Maybe," I said.

"I'll climb up the gate and see if the pipe says something about Matthew 16:18."

"Okay," said Saul, "but I do not know what good it will do. We'll still be stuck down here regardless if the lights are on or off."

Gabe hadn't heard what he said. He just kept climbing up the gate. I checked the bag to see if there might be something in there we didn't notice before. We hadn't noticed the cell phone before. I hoped something would turn up, but nothing.

"Any numbers on the pipe?" I inquired.

"Zilch," Gabe said climbing back down the steel black gate.

"Maybe we missed something upstairs in the kitchen we were supposed to grab or something. Saul, does the map give us anything else about the kitchen that we might have missed?"

"I'm pretty sure there's nothing big bro., but I'll take another look," Saul replied.

Just as I was turning toward the big wall behind us, the ladder was gone.

"Hey, where's the ladder?"

"It's right th…" Saul turned pale as he noticed it was gone, too.

"What are we looking at?" Gabe asked naïvely as he had just climbed down off the gate. Saul grabbed his head with both hands and said, "The ladder…it's gone."

"But who…wh-who…we were…how…how?" Gabe stammered.

We all frantically looked around to see if we saw anyone else down here with us. Our flashlights were bouncing all over the place, but we saw and heard no one. Assuming someone had to be behind the ladder missing, and that they probably were above us, I called out in my loudest voice, "WE KNOW YOU'RE UP THERE! SHOW YOURSELF!"

"Uh, Josh. What are you doing?" Gabe asked timidly.

I ignored him. I repeated myself just as loudly, "SHOW YOURSELF!"

Suddenly we felt our clothes blowing, graduating with more force and velocity, like a big fan was beyond the steel black gate blowing with all its might. Then a slow, creepy sounding voice starting speaking.

"**CONGRATULATIONS**," said the Voice.

We couldn't make out who the voice was. It was the first time I'd ever heard this kind of creepy voice without watching television.

The Voice continued to speak. "**NOTHING BUT PURE STUPIDITY HAS BROUGHT YOU TO THIS POINT, BUT I WILL GIVE YOU AN**

OPPORTUNITY TO EXERCISE WISDOM." At that moment, the big wall behind us had a secret door open up showing us the light from outside.

"IF YOU ARE SMART," the Voice continued speaking, "EXIT THROUGH THIS OPEN DOOR BEHIND YOU TO GO BACK TO MOMMY AND DADDY."

Gabe, without hesitation, started walking toward the door. Saul's eyes got big—shocked that Gabe wasn't even thinking clearly.

"No Gabe," I grabbed him firmly by his arm. "It's a trick."

"MAYBE YOU'RE NOT AS FOOLISH AS I PRESUMED," said the Voice.

At that, the door slowly closed until no more outside light shined through—the sound of stone hitting stone as it fully closed. The wind stopped blowing as hard.

"NO MATTER," the Voice continued, "IF YOU DO NOT MIND DEFEAT, YOU ARE CERTAINLY WELCOME TO PROCEED."

The wind stopped blowing completely. Now it was silent again—a scary kind of silent. We all stood there not knowing what to expect next.

I said, "So what are w…"

A loud continuous clanking noise started as I began to speak. We all huddled together in a startle embracing each other tightly. The large black steel gate in front of us was slowly descending into the ground. We watched it until it was no longer in sight. Down the dark hallway were torched lights on each side that lit themselves when the steel black gate was out of sight.

"Okay…um," Gabe started, "Was that *supposed* to happen?"

"Why ask why?" Saul replied.

"It could be a trick," I presumed.

"If it is a trick, what are we supposed to do?" Gabe asked. "In your own words, 'We can't go up or back'…I mean, we do not…"

"I guess you have a good point," I said interrupting as he was making his point.

Suddenly the same loud continuous clanking noise started up again. We were startled again. This time, the steel black gate was rising up out of the ground.

Using quick reflexes, I grabbed the bag and hurried my brothers along on the other side of the gate as it was rising. We had to jump over it as it slowly ascended. Before long, the steel black gate was standing tall again with no way over, around, through or under it.

"Uh…I think now would be a good time to pray," I said.

"'Couldn't have said it better myself," Saul agreed. "Let's pray."

Just as we had prayed prior to entering this dreadful house, once again, we bowed on one knee. I, of course, prayed with one eye shut and the other one open.

"Hey guys," Gabe said, "let's take out mom's mirror. Maybe there are some answers. It's the only weapon we haven't used yet."

Gabe made a good point. The map said nothing more of what we were to do next. I just do not know how mom's mirror would serve us at this present moment.

"No offense," Saul said, "but we don't have time for that."

"What else do we have?" Gabe snapped back defensively. "You have any…"

Saul snatched the mirror out of Gabe's hand.

"Let's just keep moving," Saul said sighing heavily.

Gabe reacted just as quickly and starting trying to pull it out of Saul's hand. Soon it turned into a tugglewar. Being the big brother, I jumped in the middle and snatched it off of both of them and said, "Thank you very much." The two of them just looked at each other not saying a word.

The fog that we saw outside of the house before we came inside was cropping up again, making it a little harder to see as we made our way down this hallway.

"Over a mirror, really?" I said shaking my head in unbelief because they were fighting over a mirror—over mom's pink girly mirror at that.

As I was talking, I looked down at the mirror in my hand. On the back of it was something I hadn't noticed before. It said, "Examine yourself—2 Cor. 13:5."

Examine what, I thought? Maybe our own hearts? This scripture didn't seem important to our mission, but why give us a mirror? Mom and Dad would not have placed it in the bag without a reason.

As we continued down the dark hallway with torches lit on both sides, we saw a silhouette of some object in front of us. Our flashlights were fighting through, not only the darkness, but through the smoky fog surrounding us as well. The fog seemed to be getting thicker. We started waving our hands rapidly back and forth to see past the thick smoky fog. As we drew closer...and closer...and closer... we finally were touching this silhouette. It was the BLACK CAULDRON—the black pot.

"We made it guys," Gabe said with a whole lot of excitement. "We're here. We're finally here."

Gabe hugged the black pot like it was his long-lost friend and even began kissing it—like someone who'd been drifting in the middle of the ocean for many years and finally got to land. Of course, Gabe stopped kissing and hugging the black cauldron when he realized the slimy stuff oozing down the side of it.

"O yuck," screamed Gabe. "That is *so* gross!"

As Gabe profusely wiped the black slimy stuff off of his lips and clothes, Saul and I began to circle the pot, examining it from top to bottom. The cauldron was about as tall as we were, but only barely. We were all able to look down and see the black slimy liquid inside. The cauldron resembled the same pot you see a witch standing by on Halloween posters. *All I was looking for next was a black cat to walk in the room.*

As Gabe was still wiping the slimy stuff off of himself, he flung some of it back onto the black cauldron and toward us.

"Hey, watch it," Saul snapped at Gabe.

"Sorry, but this stuff is disgusting."

"I know," Saul agreed sarcastically. "That's why I said…"

"Look at this," I interrupted.

As I was searching the cauldron with my flashlight, the spot Gabe had flung the black slimy stuff had some letters by it. I moved in for a closer look.

"What is it? What does it say?" Saul asked.

"It says," as I fumbled reading through it. "*The heart… is …deceitful …above all …things, and …incurable…; who … can… know… it? Jeremiah 17:9. THE HIDE - OUT.*"

"Beautiful job big brother," Gabe commented jokingly. "You sounded just like a broken record."

"There's "*heart*" again. It just keeps popping up," Saul said perceptively.

"This has got to be it—the heart that's haunted. This is the *haunted heart*!" I said excitedly.

I continued, "But it also says hideout. What is –"

Suddenly a black fist quickly emerged from the black slimy stuff in the black cauldron splashing the slimy stuff right onto us. My brothers and I jumped back in terror, falling down to the ground. I felt something crumble in my back pocket when I hit the ground. We scuffled back far from the black cauldron. We scuffled back until we hit what we *thought* was a wall. We shuffled and scuffled back into two strong black legs.

Moving in more panic, we scuffled to our feet, moving to the other side of the room to get away from the black figure. However, we soon figured out we were surrounded by a host of black figures. We must have been in their lair or something. There was no place we turned our heads and didn't see a black figure.

The black fist from the cauldron was a black figure as well. It emerged fully from the cauldron and just stood there looking at us—I mean, with no face and all, I guess it was looking at us. As a matter of fact, they all just looked at us, huddled tightly together with no way of busting through them. Did they know something we did not? Every other time we encountered these things, they attacked us, but this time, they just stood there.

"Uh, Josh," Gabe death-gripped my hand."Got any ideas?"

"To be honest with you little bro, I was hoping you did."

"Not the answer I was looking for," Saul chimed in.

"Flashlight!" Gabe shouted reaching for the bag, but the bag wasn't anywhere near us. We looked around and discovered that three of the many black figures had our flashlights in hand. They held up the flashlights tauntingly. Then they hurled them outside the huddled circle they made around us with the black cauldron in the middle.

We started hearing chuckles from the black faceless figures. Gabe had managed to still grab the duffle bag with the rest of our weapons.

As we looked around the room at each black figure, we noticed each one had a sinful name written on their chest in bright green neon letters. I saw BLASPHEMY, EVIL THOUGHTS, SORCERY, IDOLATRY, DRUNKENNESS, HATRED and JEALOUSY.

I still had the mirror in my hand. Even with falling, I managed to hold on to it without it breaking. My brothers and I started huddling tightly together with our backs touching firmly. I wielded the mirror like a sword—unintentionally of course—and to my surprise I saw the black figures turning away their "faceless" faces as if they didn't want to look at us, or at least their own "faceless" faces in the mirror.

"What's going on?" Saul asked perplexingly.

"I don't know," I replied hastily. "Just stick together."

At that, I started moving slightly closer to a couple of black figures. As we moved closer, they moved further back. It must be the mirror that scares them, but why? Yet and still, I continued to circle my way around the room holding the mirror closer and closer to each black figure. As expected, as we moved closer with the mirror, they all moved back.

Thinking about the crushing sensation in my pocket, I discreetly handed the mirror to Saul and told him to continue holding up the mirror for our protection. I reached in my back pocket and pulled it out.

"What are you doing with that pouch?" Gabe asked very curiously.

"Remember that black pouch Dad put in my hand?"

"Yeah."

"I think this is it."

"What is it?"

"This mission," Saul replied understanding what the pouch was for.

"I don't get it. Can someone explain it to–"

"It is finished," I said interrupting Gabe with confidence. Without hesitation I, then, opened the black pouch and poured the contents inside the cauldron.

To my surprise, nothing happened. The black slimy stuff absorbed the contents from the pouch—like it swallowed it whole.

"Now what?" I asked aloud.

"**WHAT ARE YOU DOING?**" asked the Voice in a hissing manner.

We looked all around the room for the voice because we couldn't figure out where it was coming from. It seemed to be coming from everywhere.

The Voice continued to speak, "**YOU KNOW THERE IS NO WAY OUT OF HERE. YOU SHOULD'VE LEFT WHEN YOU HAD THE CHANCE. YOU CAN RUN, BUT YOU CANNOT HIDE.**"

"Hide," I repeated.

"Hide?" Saul and Gabe asked together with confusion.

"Yes, hide," I repeated with more enthusiasm.

They both looked at each other even more confused.

"Remember the Hiding Place at home?" The cauldron has engraved on it, "**THE HIDE - OUT**."

"Gabe," I said, "don't you get it?"

"Get what?" he asked with more confusion.

"Like at home, Gabe," Saul jumped in. "The same way we put our Scriptures in the Hiding Place at home."

Gabe looked down at the ground thinking and then saw a pipe running across it. He kept looking at the pipe, followed it until it finally led to…

"My memory verse!" Gabe exclaimed. The pipe led right to the black cauldron, which was a part of it.

"**GET THEM!**" said the Voice loudly. "**ATTACK!**"

The black figures started moving in quickly. We continued to keep our backs pressed against each other, Saul still wielding the mirror.

"Gabe," said Saul. "Get that love bomb out."

"I'm trying!" Gabe yelled struggling to get it out. "The zipper's stuck!"

"Josh, do something," Saul raised his voice. "I can't do this forever."

I grabbed the duffle bag and tore it open. I reached in and grabbed his charitable explosive and the 3C Detonator. I gave the charitable explosive to Gabe. We continued to move closer to the black cauldron until Gabe was facing it. With only the 3C Detonator in hand, I only prayed one of these strong black figures wouldn't take it off of me. Otherwise we would be doomed.

It seemed like years were passing by waiting for Gabe to quote his memory verse. The Voice continued to barrage ominous words at us. The black figures seemed to be getting closer. Their hands were extended, waiting for a moment to grab our weapons off of us with the slightest loss of attention. Finally, though, I heard the charitable explosive latch to the pipe. I must have been so focused on protecting us from these black monsters and fighting off the words of the Voice with good thoughts, I didn't even hear him cite his verse.

"Quick," yelled Saul, "hit the button!"

You know how everything goes dark when something major is about to happen? Well, in this situation, after I hit the button, everything went bright—super bright. It was so bright I couldn't see anything.

Now while I couldn't see anything, I could hear a whole lot of noise. I heard the noise of footsteps running away from the area we were. I heard the Voice speaking, but I couldn't make out what it was saying. The Voice sounded surprised that it'd been beaten. Its voice sounded digitally broken as it spoke in a slow fade until I could no longer hear it. "*NOOOOooooooooooooo...!*"

As the bright light dimmed, we saw another silhouette, except this time, it was the silhouette of a woman. We held our hands over our eyes slightly to block out some light and to get a better view of this woman standing before us.

The smoky fog was clearing out as well. After it was completely gone, we finally saw the woman who was standing before us. In a very soft-spoken voice and with a big smile, she slowly started walking toward us.

Our countenances really lit up when we realized that it was the one and only best Bible teacher of all time, Mrs. Paraclete. We ran up to her exuberantly. Every happy and joyous moment we ever had in this dreadful house seemed to all come together at the moment we embraced Mrs. Paraclete. She embraced us back seeming to understand that we'd been through a great deal of…well…more than any one should have to go through before they turn thirteen.

We were so glad to see her that none of us even questioned why she was here in the house. I was about to speak up but she started talking before I could.

"You boys were so brave in here, especially you Gabe. You are only 9 years—"

"Nine and a half Mrs. Paraclete…*nine* and a half," Gabe gently corrected her.

"I'm so sorry," Mrs. Paraclete said laughingly and apologetically. "Forgive me Father for I have sinned."

"But you knew," Gabe said looking up at her. "You knew since this morning at Church."

"This morning?" came a voice asking in the distance. We all looked back to see who was talking to us.

"Mom…Dad!" I exclaimed happily recognizing them both walking toward us.

Gabe bounced from Mrs. Paraclete straight over to mom very swiftly, embracing her tightly.

"This morning," Dad continued gleefully. "She's known for months."

"Months," Saul said surprised. "You all were a part of this—for months?"

"Months," mom answered rubbing Gabe's head affectionately.

I was shocked at the answer, too. I had a feeling Mom and Dad were behind all of this, but not to this extent.

"You mean to tell us," I started speaking, "that you were responsible for those black faceless figures?"

"Well how else were we going to get you to see the *true value* of remembering your Bible verses?" Dad replied answering my question with a question, but not really *answering* my question. Naturally I was confused and so were my brothers.

Dad started walking the room and began explaining to us all that we had been through in this...(ahem)... *haunted*... heart.

"You know how I always say," Dad began, "'we are creatures of forgetfulness, but memory is a skill. So choose to _not_ forget?'"

We all nodded our heads in agreement.

"We *forget*," Dad said looking at each of us pointing at his own head and ours, "because what's in our heads never makes it to our hearts."

"However," Dad continued pointing at our chests and his own, "we *remember* because what's in our hearts is no longer in our heads."

Our expression was blank. None of us knew where Dad was going with this head and heart talk. Thankfully, mom joined in on the conversation.

"You know the Hiding Place in the dining room?"

Again, we nodded our heads in agreement.

"Well," mom continued, "do any of you remember the words on it?"

We stood there trying to think of what words were on the crystal-shaped heart on the dining room table, but we all shrugged our shoulders upward with our palms up. None of us knew.

"It says, 'Thy word have I hid in my heart,'" mom pointed at our chests, "'that I might not sin against Thee.' Psalm 119:11."

"Okay?" Saul inquired in a perplexed manner.

"When you put Bible verses in your heart," Mom continued, "you won't do bad things God doesn't like… and…you save a dark haunted heart from darkness by bringing the light…of God's love."

Mrs. Paraclete helped out and pointed to the cauldron that was no longer black, but filled with light.

"You saved it from darkness," she said. "This whole *heart* is full of light."

"All of this was possible because you remembered your Bible memory verses from this morning," Mom chimed in.

"Do you get it now," Dad asked enthusiastically. "Those charitable explosives were shaped like hearts and had your memory verses programmed inside."

All they were saying was starting to become clearer, to me at least.

"So what you're saying," I attempted to make sense of all they were saying, "is we do not remember our Bible verses for a treat –"

"But to treat someone with your memory verse," Mrs. Paraclete finished my sentence.

"So the 'someone' we were treating," I continued, "was… was…"

"This haunted heart," Dad said. "This haunted heart represents all the unbelievers in the world. Your only job was to bring God's word—*your memory verses* - and love to it—*that's the charitable explosives and the 3C Detonator.*"

"So does this mean," Gabe said with great comprehension and compassion, "that we are not going to get our JELL-O Dirt Cups?"

Mom, Dad and Mrs. Paraclete started to chuckle at Gabe's response, but never answered him. Gabe was looking bewildered as they laughed.

"So when God's word, or Bible verses are in *your heart*, you will never forget them," Dad said. "So we choose to not forget when we commit Bible verses to our hearts. Committing Bible verses to our heads just isn't enough. There, they can be forgotten."

"What about the three fears we had to face? What's that have to do with everything you're saying?" Saul asked.

"Telling people about God's love is never easy," mom said. "We have to not be afraid to stand up for God and be brave. The devil or Emperor Hamartia tried to use fear to keep you all from finishing this assignment we gave you."

"That's why you gave us that Joshua Scripture and those three fears of faith?" Saul said starting to figure it out.

"Right," she said. "We used Halloween this year—a holiday about scary stuff - as an opportunity to show you to face your fear. The three fears of faith aren't really fear but respecting three different things—God, fear itself and sin's power."

"So each time we prayed," Saul said, "we respected God's power."

"Right again," mom said. "You showed you understood God's power was stronger than your own. By using your flashlights and praying, you also recognized that the power of sin—the black faceless figures—were stronger than you, but NOT stronger than God.

"That's why they ran away from us when we shined the lights on them," I said.

Mom and Dad were nodding in agreement with what I was saying.

"Yeah," Saul said, "Dad said, 'Darkness cannot stand light.'"

"Right," Dad said. "Sin—which is what the black faceless figures represented—never wants to be exposed. They thrive in the dark."

"Is anyone hearing me, "Gabe asked uninterested in everything we were all talking about. "Are we going to get our treats?"

Dad, mom and Mrs. Paraclete just laughed again.

"Why didn't you tell us about the cell phone? You told us about everything else," I asked my Dad.

"I thought it was obvious. You never found the charger, did you?" Dad replied.

"No," Saul and I said as we looked at each other, and then watched as Dad pulled the cell phone charger out of his pocket.

"If you knew about the phone before you were supposed to, you might have tried to call us and never got that important call from your teacher."

"Okay, enough of the my-ster-ster…ious theat…the-at," Gabe jumped in and interrupted, and stuttering like crazy.

"Mysterious theatrics," I helped Gabe out unable to hold back my little chuckle.

"Whatever! Are we getting our JELL-O Dirt Cups or what?"

"Okay," Mrs. Paraclete finally acknowledged him, "as promised, let's go and get those JELL-O Dirt Cups."

With excitement Gabe said, "I am so glad to be getting out of this house –"

"Heart," Mrs. Paraclete corrected him.

"Whatever," Gabe said smiling. "We're still getting out of here."

The slimy stuff that was black was now bright neon white. Dad had taken a cross about as tall as my brothers and I. He, then, placed it in the cauldron.

"Why are you putting that cross in the cauldron, Dad," Gabe asked now seeming interested.

"Because Emperor Hamartia is no longer the ruler of this heart," Saul answered for Dad.

"Well, then who is," Gabe asked.

"Jesus Christ, of course," I said in a matter of fact way.

Dad asked us, "You guys want to do this next year? We can—"

"No, no no," we interrupted him.

"Okay," Dad said, "but you guys should know something."

"What's that?" I asked.

Mom gently grabbed my head with both of her hands, looked me square in my eyes and said, "The *mind* may easily forget things, but it can also be a very…very…very…very… dangerous place."

Dangerous place, I thought. What is she talking about? She didn't seem to be pushing it too much, so I didn't bother asking what she meant. Besides, I can really go for a JELL-O Dirt Cup. I think we've worked hard for it.

"Okay with the riddles," Gabe said. "I'm ready for JELL-O Dirt Cups. It's time to celebrate!"

"Well, you know you will not get the treat until next Sunday?" Mrs. Paraclete reminded us.

"Okay, can you at least give us the recipe for JELL-O Dirt Cups," we asked.

"Sure," she said.

As we walked out of the brightly lit house…excuse me… heart, I took a glance back at the house and saw the attic go dark. My heart dropped for a minute until I saw the light come back on. I was relieved.

As we continued to walk home, Saul nudged me with his shoulder, and kind of whispered, "You know the lights are out up in the attic?"

"No they're not," I answered quickly. "I just saw them come back on."

"No big bro.," Saul came back. "They're off."

As I was getting ready to turn around to look, Gabe showed me the recipe to the JELL-O Dirt Cups, completely distracting me from Saul's words and distracting Saul himself.

Thinking of the treat we'd soon be munching on, I took notice of all the trick-or-treaters going from house to house, wearing all kinds of different costumes and gathering their treats for later. Funny, these trick-or-treaters visit houses to *get* treats, but we visited a *heart* to give it the greatest treat.

A YEAR LATER

Saul and I were reminiscing about last year how our parents 'conspired' with Mrs. Paraclete to send us into a haunted house…(Ahem)…heart…to help us memorize our Bible memory verses and to see that they work in everyday life.

We talked of it joyously because it was all behind us—a story we can tell our grandkids when we're gray and old.

Of course, now I'm 13 years old—a teenager y'all! I'm three years away from getting my driver's license! I already know what kind of car I want.

On our way home from school on the school bus, Saul and I (*Gabe wasn't with us—he is still in grade school*) saw the house Mom and Dad made us go to.

"Look, Saul," I said pointing at the house.

"Yeah," Saul said looking where I was pointing.

"What were you saying before about the attic last year? I got side-tracked when Gabe showed us the ingredients to those JELL-O Dirt Cups." I asked.

"The lights are out…still," Saul said.

"Still?"

"Yeah," Saul said. "They've been out all y –"

Suddenly we saw Mom and Dad going in the house—the same dreadful house we were in last year.

"What do you think they're up to this year?" Saul asked intriguingly.

"No idea, little bro. Absolutely no idea whatsoever," I responded.

On the school bus, we were at a red light. Other kids on the bus had their own conversations going. Then the light turned green but the bus driver never moved the bus. I didn't pay it too much attention, but after several minutes, the driver still hadn't moved.

The whole bus was now starting to get restless. One kid started to speak up and say something to the bus driver. The bus driver was still non-responsive. So I thought to myself to go up to the bus driver and have a few words of my own.

"Excuse me, sir," I addressed the bus driver. "We've been sitting at this light for a long time now. Everyone's honking their horns behind us. Are you okay?"

Now I hadn't seen his face because for some strange reason, he tilted his rearview mirror up facing the ceiling. Since being at the light, he'd been looking down in his lap the entire time.

Then the driver turned his face toward me, and said, "Your parents just texted me on my phone. They want you to get off here at this stop—you and your brother."

"Mrs. Paraclete!" I whispered loudly. I was confused. I couldn't believe it. Not only does our Bible teacher teach, but she drives, too!

Normally our bus driver is a guy, but I thought it was kind of weird getting on the bus from school that our regular driver looked kind of pretty. Then I heard the official message on the two-way radio.

"Dispatch to bus number T321. Do you copy?" said the lady on the two-way radio.

"T321, loud and clear, go ahead dispatch," Mrs. Paraclete responded.

"Two students on your bus: Joshua and Saul Messiash; their parents are requesting you drop them off at the intersection of Transformation Ave and Mind St. You copy?" came the lady's voice from the two-way radio.

"Copy," replied Mrs. Paraclete.

It just so happened that we were on Transformation Ave. and Mind St. right now.

Saul had walked up to me and said, "Are we getting–?"

Saul gasped, "– Mrs. Paraclete!"

"Greetings Saul," she said with her big smile.

We both looked kind of bewildered. So I asked the next obvious question.

"What are you doing here?" I asked with a tone of surprise.

"I thought it was obvious," she said smiling.

"And what is that exactly, holding up traffic?" Saul said smiling back.

"No silly," she replied, "getting you where you need to go."

Thinking about last year, 'where we needed to go'—I mean, worst case scenario—was probably back in the house we saw Mom and Dad go into only moments ago.

"That's exactly right," she said.

My eyes got bigger than ever. Could she truly read minds? I think she just read mine.

"Can you hear my thoughts?"

"Thoughts?" she replied to me perplexed.

"She'd have to be God himself to hear your thoughts," Saul chimed in.

"But I was *just* thinking that we needed to go back into that house we were in last year," I rambled on, "and then as I thought it –

"Easy, Josh," she said pointing at her ear. "I'm also talking to your Mom on the other end on my cell. I have a wireless headset in my ear, see? The last thing I said, I said to your Mom."

"Oh," I said relieved.

She then said to both us, "I wouldn't get too comfortable, though, if I were you."

"Why is that?" asked Saul.

"Once again," she said, "I thought it was obvious."

We looked at each other knowing, and yet hoping that what we knew wasn't true.

As fate would have it, however, what we wished wasn't true, turned out to be what we dreaded—*true.* After coming off the bus and safely crossing both streets, and the school bus drove off, we were standing in the front of that dreadful place we were last year, except this time a banner was stretched across the entire house reading: **DANGEROUS MIND.**

FEAR NOTHING BUT GOD AND TAKE THIS HOLIDAY AS AN OPPORTUNITY TO SHOW HIS LOVE TO THOSE WHO LOVE THIS TIME OF THE YEAR.

OUTRO

Before this book *was* a book, it was a short simple story I wrote for my oldest three children back in 2006. I was trying to think of an alternative to do for Halloween that year. I decided to create my own story fused with traditional Halloween family-friendly scary stuff with a *serious* Christian twist.

I also decided to make the story visual and kinesthetic. We turned our house into a haunted house…(Ahem… excuse me)…*Heart*…to really put them in the story—to bring the story to life.

I went all out for this occasion. We had the house pitched black. I went to Paper Mart and Party City to grab different items—plastic black pot/cauldron, CD with scary sounds and music of Halloween, mini-fog creator to put in the pot to create smoke and even all the ingredients for the JELL-O Dirt Cups– actually my wife purchased and made the JELL-O Dirt Cups.

Well, after writing my first book, *How to be a Super Man for your Wife* in 2007, I realized that I could put a little more than 7-10 pages to this story. As I fiddled around with it, it became more…and more…and more…well over a hundred pages.

So you are reading a book that is 5-6 years in the making and it all started just wanting to bless my family for the cause of Christ.

So I write this for the parents out there who want to give a nice Christian-themed alternative for this Halloween season (*or whatever time of the year you are giving this book away as a gift or something*). I write this for the kids who love to read. I write this for the kids who want something infused with a rich message where nothing is without meaning. I write this to the kids who want the scary stuff but can still get the Christian message.

More than anything, I write this book as a tribute to all of my children (all six of them) to keep Christ at the center of their lives for the *rest* of their lives. Let any and every holiday, especially Halloween, be an opportunity to share the love of Christ.

Lastly to my children, never be afraid to love the unreached, the lost and the broken. They may act as if they enjoy the darkness, but nothing could be further from the truth. Those whose hearts are *desperately* wicked are *desperately* crying out for the Light.

JELL-O DIRT CUPS RECIPE

(Ingredients & Instructions)

1 package (16 ounces) of **chocolate sandwich cookies** or Oreo cookies

2 cups of cold milk

1 package (4-serving size) **JELL-O Chocolate flavor Instant Pudding and Pie Filling.**

1 tub (8 ounces) of **COOL WHIP**, whipped topping thawed

8-10 (7-ounce) paper or plastic cups

Decorations: **Gummy worms** and frogs, Candy flowers, chopped peanuts, and Granola

Crush cookies in zipper-style plastic bag with rolling pin or in food processor.

Pour milk in large bowl. Add pudding mix. Beat with wire whisk 1 to 2 minutes. Let it stand for 5 minutes. Stir in whipped topping and ½ of the crushed cookies.

Place about 1 tablespoon crushed cookies into each cup. Fill cups about ¾ full with pudding mixture. Top with remaining crushed cookies.

Refrigerate 1 hour or until ready to serve. Decorate with gummy worms and frogs, candy flowers, peanuts and granola.

Makes 8-10 servings.

THE SUBLIMINAL MESSAGES
OF THIS BOOK

Mrs. Paraclete:

The Holy Spirit. Paraclete is the Greek word for Comforter, which means "another of the same kind," referring to the essence of God.

Joshua:

Jesus Christ. Joshua is also the original Hebrew form of the Greek name Jesus. The name means "God saves."

Gabe & Saul:

Followers of Christ. Gabe means "strong man of God." He is named Gabe because he loves standing in his mother's presence as the angel Gabriel stands in the presence of God. The name 'Saul' (from *Sha'ul*) is the Hebrew name for "pray," which means something asked for or requested.

The Greatest Treat:

The gospel of Jesus Christ

The Hiding Place:	**Our hearts** where we hide or place God's word. Scripture says, "Thy word have I hid in my heart, so I will not sin against You" (Psalm 119:11). When we safeguard His word in our most precious place, He safeguards us from sinning.
Our Parents:	**God the Father**. As appears in Scripture and from the lips of Jesus, Father God orders the missions we serve. Jesus said that the Father sent Him.
House:	an **evil sinful heart**. The story indicates that we, like the house, are alive yet lifeless. The Bible says we were once dead in trespasses and sins. That is, we were alive yet dead because our hearts were dark by sin.
Light:	light of truth; of **God's word**
Black Cauldron:	Unbelief: an evil **sinful heart (at the core)** *see house*.
Mom's Mirror:	**God's word**. James 1:23-26. It shows us ourselves.
Flashlight:	**God's word**. Psalm 119:105. It guides us along the way.
Map:	**God's word**. Psalm 119:133. It maps the way for us.
Charitable Explosives:	**showing love** where it matters most
3C Detonator:	**willingness to show love**. Choosing Charity Constantly

<u>Little Black Pouch</u>:	**Sinner's prayer**: *I surrender my heart to you Jesus. I admit that my heart is haunted and ruled by sin. You are the only one who can save me from the darkness of sin and bring Your light of love to a heart longing so desperately for You.*

<u>3 Fears of Faith</u>:

1) **Respect God** 2) **Respect Fear**
3) **Respect Sin**

The fears of faith aren't fear as in terror, but fear as in respect, awe or reverence. In order to bring the gospel to others we have to respect God and His power—that His power is stronger than any power in the world, that He can bring light to all darkness, no matter how great that darkness!

Jesus told us that we should not be afraid of people who can only kill the body, but in awe of God who can destroy both body and soul in hell. So we need to respect the power of fear by not being afraid or giving into fear. The Bible says, "There is no fear in love. Perfect (or mature) love removes all fear because fear has torment (or terror)" (1 John 4:18). We must respect the power of sin knowing that we cannot conquer it with our own power. Only God's power through the gospel message of Christ can triumph over it.

<u>Hamartia Diablo:</u>	**Satan**. *Hamartia* is the Greek word for *sin* and *diablo* is the Greek word for *devil*. By the title "Emperor," it indicates that the devil and sin are ruling the heart, making it evil, dark and sinful.
<u>Black Figures:</u>	**different types of sin** in our hearts. The words on their chests represent what sin they are (Matthew 15:19).
<u>The Perish Room:</u>	a **key area of the heart** to show God's love
<u>Brewing Death:</u>	**sins**
<u>Gas Masks:</u>	represent us forgiving those who have sinned against us, **looking past their faults** as Christ does in order to save them. For "love covers a multitude of sins" (1 Peter 4:8).
<u>Gates of Hell:</u>	a **key area of the heart** to show God's love and bring His marvelous light

FOR THE SINNER WHOSE HEART IS HAUNTED

What about your heart? Is it haunted with sin? If it is, God wants to come in and bring His glorious light, love and life-changing Word inside.

God, like the father in this story sending his own children to a haunted heart, has sent His children to bring the gospel of Jesus Christ to your haunted, sin-filled heart—to bring God's light, love and life-changing Word.

It could've been a family member, someone in your community or neighborhood, a classmate at school or maybe even a friend trying to tell you about Jesus Christ.

God loves haunted hearts and wants to enter in for the sheer thrill of it, and bring joy to you as well. The Bible says, "The angels rejoice over one sinner (*someone with a haunted heart*) that repents" (Luke 15:10).

God isn't afraid of your dark, spooky, haunted and sin-filled heart. He's more than up for the challenge to stay inside your haunted heart for as long as it takes to bring you into the glorious light of the gospel of Jesus Christ (2 Corinthians 4:3-4).

FOR THOSE TRYING TO BRING THE GOSPEL LIGHT TO HAUNTED HEARTS

Telling other people about Jesus Christ isn't as hard as you think. Reaching out to people with the gospel is really simple.

This story you just read, *Haunted Heart: The 3 Fears of Faith*, lays out effective evangelism to bringing the gospel to people with haunted hearts ruled by sin.

Chapter one tells us that the greatest treat is not candy for your tummy, but the gospel for haunted hearts. Chapter two tells that haunted hearts love darkness rather than light (John 3:16-19).

Notice in the story how there are three memory Scriptures talking about the love of God, and how each of them are set as explosives in certain rooms of the house to shed the most light. It's the love of God that draws people to Christ, to salvation (Jeremiah 31:3).

This teaches us that we must be strategic in how we love others. Love them in a way that is effective. Each person is different so you must pay attention to love them accordingly.

Remember the 3 fears of faith: revere **God**, respect **sin** and respect the *power of fear?* God is all powerful; sin is stronger than you but less powerful than God and you must face your fear instead of giving into it. *Don't be afraid to tell people about Jesus because He's stronger than their sin.* The Bible says, "Do not fear people who can only kill your body; rather, fear God who can destroy both your body and soul in Hell" (Matthew 10:28).

The people who should really be afraid are those who hearts are haunted with sin, not you whose heart is no longer haunted by sin, but occupied by the Holy Spirit.

Chapter three tells us that sin is much stronger than us and we stand no chance against it unless we have the light of God's truth and Word to fight against it. Chapter four shows that, like God, we must love people past the smelly foul odor of their sin.

Chapter 5 shows us that it is Jesus Christ who makes a haunted heart a holy heart (1 Corinthians 3:6). The mirror represents God's Word to help people see their own sin so that they repent and turn to Jesus.

FUN FACTS

Here are all the <u>years</u> Halloween fell on a Sunday since 1971 & something significant that happened each of these years.

1971
The **Pittsburgh Pirates** won the World Series against the Baltimore Orioles this year

1976
The **M&M Candy Company** stopped putting *red M&M's* in the bag until 1987

1982
This is the same year **Ben Roethlisberger** (quarterback for Pittsburgh Steelers) was born.

1993
This is the same year **I gave my life to Jesus Christ** just before entering high school

1999
A total **solar eclipse** happened August 11. The moon's shadow started at the Atlantic Ocean.

2004
This was the same year a "**leap year**" occurred

2010
This is the same year *Toy Story 3* **hit the theaters**.

THE NEXT TIME HALLOWEEN WILL FALL ON A SUNDAY WILL BE IN THE YEAR 2021

If you would like to get in contact with me, my e-mail is Insulated4Christ@gmail.com. Feel free to ask me questions, make suggestions or comments about this book anytime. In the event that I receive a large volume of emails, please give me up to 2—4 weeks for a response, and 1—2 weeks for a response if the volume is low.

Also, if you would like to book me for speaking engagements, book signings, radio, T.V. appearances etc., feel free to contact this email address.

I will give you all details for booking information over e-mail. I'm very flexible and not hungry for money. I'm all about the message of Christ being proclaimed. I will work with you as much as possible, but do not get that twisted with "no compensation" and covering necessary fees and costs.

Here is one last very important detail. If you want to book me for an event, I need a month's notice for the date you are requesting my presence. For example, if you need me to attend an event you are hosting on February 6, 2014, it needs to be confirmed between the two of us ON or BEFORE January 6, 2014.

God bless you, and I look forward to speaking with you soon.

Sincerely in His name,

Jerry H.